"Jory Sh...
Nationa...
Loren D....

The Walker Colt seemed to spring into Zak's hand.

He looked down a long dark tunnel as the pistol exploded, gushing flame and lead, bucking in his hand. At the end of the tunnel, Felipe, in stark relief, was hammering back for a second shot. Zak's .44 caliber ball of soft lead struck him just below his rib cage with the force of a sledgehammer. Dust flew from his shirt, and a black hole appeared like a quick wink that filled suddenly with blood.

The hammered bullet drove Felipe off his moorings and he staggered backward, slamming into the wall of the adobe. He gasped for air and slid down the wall, his fingers turning limp, the pistol drooping, then falling from his grasp.

Zak stepped toward Felipe, his pistol at full cock for another shot, if needed. Smoke spooled from the barrel as he knelt down in front of Felipe.

"I won't say adios to you," Zak said, his voice a soft rasp, just above a whisper. "God isn't going with you on this journey. He's just going to watch you fall into a deep hole. The next sound you hear will be me. Walking over your grave, you sonofabitch."

By Jory Sherman

SHADOW RIDER
BLOOD SKY AT MORNING

JORY SHERMAN

HARPER

An Imprint of HarperCollinsPublishers

HARPER

An Imprint of HarperCollins*Publishers*
10 East 53rd Street
New York, New York 10022-5299

Copyright © 2007 by Jory Sherman
ISBN: 978-0-06-088528-1
ISBN-10: 0-06-088528-9

First Harper paperback printing: March 2007

HarperCollins® and Harper® are registered trademarks of HarperCollins Publishers.

Printed in the U.S.A.

10 9 8 7 6 5 4

For Arlie Weir

SHADOW RIDER
BLOOD SKY AT MORNING

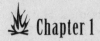 Chapter 1

Zak Cody cut sign that morning just after he passed
Dos Cabezas. The tracks were both disturbing and
puzzling. There was blood, too, mixed in with the
dirt and the rocks. At least six men, he figured, on
unshod ponies, had lain in wait for the stagecoach.
There were drag marks, and these led him to a
gruesome discovery.

The bodies of two men lay spread-eagled on their
backs near a clump of mesquite and cholla. Their
throats were cut, gaping like hideous grins. Blue-
bottles and blowflies crawled over the wounds and
clustered on their eyes. The men were hatless and
scalped. They wore army uniforms and they had
been stripped of their sidearms.

Zak stepped off his horse to examine the dead
men more closely. One of them, a young lieutenant
with blond fuzz still on his face, had blood on his
shirt, a few inches under his armpit. He pulled the
shirttail out and saw the wound. It appeared the
young man had been stabbed there. The other man
wore a sergeant's chevrons on his shirt. He had a
dragoon moustache and there were small scars on
his face that had long since healed. A fighter, from

the looks of him. His nose had been broken at least
once in his lifetime, which Zak judged to have been
about forty years.

Moccasin tracks all around the bodies. Hard to
tell the tribe. Chiricahua maybe. This was their
country. The hair on both men's heads appeared
to have been pulled back to take their scalps, slit
their throats. A few strands around the dollar-size
patch where the scalps had been lifted were sticking straight up.

At least one of the men had voided when he died.
The young lieutenant, he decided, when he bent
over to sniff. He smelled like a latrine. The urine
smell stung his nostrils, so they hadn't been dead
long. An hour, maybe less.

He set about deciphering the tracks, walking
around the wagon's marks where it had stopped.
Wagon or stagecoach, he couldn't tell for sure
which just then. Six separate sets of horse tracks.
Four horses, shod, pulling the wagon or coach. A
depression where one body had fallen, close to the
side. The driver, probably. On the other side, more
marks, indicating a struggle, then another depression a few feet away from the wagon tracks.

Then the wagon had driven off. And it wasn't
trailing any of the unshod horses. Who had been
driving? Why had he or they been allowed to leave?
Was the lieutenant the target? The sergeant? Both?
Strange, Zak thought.

He mounted up and continued down the road in
the direction the wagon had gone. The pony tracks
led off on another tangent. Business finished. Where
had they gone? There was no way to tell without
following the tracks. And even then, he might not

know why they had attacked the wagon, or coach, and why they had just let it drive off. None inside the wagon had stepped down. He had accounted for all the tracks.

Yet someone had escaped.

Why?

Zak touched a hand to his face. Two days of stubble stippled his jaw. The hairs were stiff enough to make a sound like someone scraping a match head across sandpaper. He touched spurs to his horse's flanks and left the smell of death behind.

The wind moved miniature dust devils across the land like dervishes on a giant chess board, with squares painted burnt umber and yellow ochre. Cloud shadows slipped across the rocky outcroppings and small spires like wraiths from some surreal dream, slinking and rippling over the contours of the desolate earth, making the land seem to pulse and breathe. Little lakes shimmered and vanished in the smoke of shadows, only to reappear again farther on in silver curtains that danced enticingly along the old Butterfield Stage route that wound through stone cairns and cactus like the fossilized path of an ancient serpent grown to gigantic size.

Zak Cody licked the black cracks on his lips, shifted the pebble in his mouth from one side to the other. His canteen was empty, all of the water inside him where it could oil his muscles, saturate his tendons. That was the Apache way, not the white man's, who rationed water until he died of thirst, leaving his gaunt skeleton on the desert either through ignorance or an addled mind.

He found the first object beside the trail almost by accident. A glint of sun, something odd seen out of the corner of his eye. He rode over to see what was glittering so, thinking it a stone veined with mica or quartz. But there was a blue-green cast to it that defied immediate identification. It was small, and might have passed notice on an overcast day.

He reined in the black and dismounted. Stooping down, he picked up the dazzling object, turned it over in his fingers while he stared at it. There was gold on it, too, and he saw that it was a piece of jewelry. Woman's jewelry. The gold band was attached to the precious stone, and there was a pointed shaft through the band. A woman's earring, he determined, before he put it in his shirt pocket. A few feet away, almost hidden from view, he spotted the matching earring. He slid it into his pocket with the other one and climbed back into the saddle.

Now, what would a woman, possibly a refined woman, be doing way out in the middle of nowhere, miles from any sizable town, any town where a fine lady might wear such a fashionable accessory? Ahead, miles away still, was Apache Springs, and beyond that, Fort Bowie. He had seen the wagon tracks, knew how fresh they were, how many horses, four, were pulling it, and how fast they were going. Cody was a tracker, by both habit and training, so he always studied the ground wherever he rode his black gelding, a Missouri trotter, sixteen hands high. He called the horse Nox, knowing it was the Latin word for night.

A hawk floated over the road, dragging its rumpled shadow after it along the ground. It disappeared over a rise and a moment later he heard its shrill *scree scree*. The sound faded into the long silence of the desert, and then he heard only Nox's shod hooves striking the hard ground.

A few moments later, he figured perhaps fifteen minutes had passed, he saw something else that was out of place in such surroundings. A flash of silver light bounced off it in one short streak, almost like a falling star going in the wrong direction, from earth to the heavens. He stopped and picked it up.

A bracelet, of silver and turquoise. Probably Tasco silver, from the way it was wrought, so finely turned, turquoise beads embedded in round casings that clasped them tight. A woman's bracelet, graceful and elegant, such as a refined lady might wear.

Zak crossed and recrossed the ruts in the ground, looking for more cast-off artifacts. Ten minutes later he found a necklace made of silver and turquoise, like the bracelet. He stopped long enough to retrieve it and put it in his pocket before he rode on. He kept his gaze on the broken land, scanning both sides of the road for any sign of movement, judging the age of the tracks, holding Nox to a steady, ground-eating pace, closing the distance between him and the four-wheeled vehicle.

He spat out the pebble when Nox gave a low whicker and his ears stiffened to cones, twisted in a semiarc. Apache Springs was close, he knew, and he began to drift wide of the road, but keeping it in sight. The tracks were very fresh now, and as he topped a small rise, the springs lay below him, a wide spot in the road, deserted except for the small coach that stood off to one side. A woman sat on the seat, alone, her head facing the opposite way.

He saw legs move between the horses. A man was checking the traces.

Zak rode toward the coach, his hazel eyes narrowed to thin dark slits. They flickered with little flecks of gold and light brown, specks of magenta. The man emerged from between the horse's legs, and the woman turned and stared straight at him. A hand went up to her mouth and she stiffened on the seat.

"Ho there," Zak called as he rode down to the springs, wending his way through the ocotillo and prickly pear. There was a legend painted on the side of the coach: FERGUSON'S STAGE AND FREIGHT COMPANY. Underneath, in smaller letters: HAULING, PASSENGER SERVICE. And, in still smaller letters: *Hiram Ferguson, Prop.* Zak had seen such before. Ferguson operated out of Tucson, ran lines down to Bisbee, over to Vail and up to Safford. He sometimes connected with freight out of Tucson, since he went places nobody much wanted to go in that part of the country.

The man stepped away from the horses. He was wearing a linen duster, pale yellow in color, and his hat brim was folded to a funnel that shielded his eyes.

"Howdy, stranger," the man said. "See any hostiles?"

Zak looked at the woman, then back at the man. Suspicion crept through his mind like some small night creature, sniffing, probing, twitching its whiskers. Something about the way the man was standing, the way he held his arms out, slightly bowed, away from his sides. And the woman, just in that brief glance, seemed paralyzed with fear. Fear was something Zak could almost smell, as if it gave off a scent, more subtle than sweat but as distinctive as fumes from a burning match.

"Hostiles?" Zak slowed his horse, halted it a few feet from the man, the coach, the cowering woman.

"You know. Apaches. We run into a hell of a patch back there."

The man inclined his head in the direction that the coach had come from. Zak noticed he didn't lift a hand to point a finger.

"No," Zak said. "I saw no Apaches."

"Well, they's about."

Zak reached into his pocket, fingered the bracelet. He pulled it out, dangled it like bait on a hook from his left index finger. He looked straight at the woman.

"You lose this?" he said.

The woman uttered a small breathy "Oh," and her face drained of color. She glanced quickly at the man on the ground, the man in the duster, standing at the head of the four horses.

"She didn't lose nothin'," the man said, and he glanced up at the woman. The look he gave her was so quick it might have escaped notice from the average person. But Zak caught it. He caught the warning, the puzzlement. "Well, now, she might have," the man said. "Where'd you find it?"

"I asked *her*," Zak said, his voice flat as a leaf spring.

Zak moved the bracelet up and down. Lances of bright light shot from its faceted surface as he twirled it to catch the sun.

"Or maybe you lost this," Zak said, fishing one of the earrings from the same pocket. "Or this, the other one." He held up the second earring.

The woman rubbed her wrist. It was paler than the rest of her skin, a place where a bracelet might have been worn. Then she touched her neck.

Zak put the other pieces back in his pocket, pulled out the necklace. He dangled it like some gewgaw he was hawking, his gaze taking in both the man and the woman.

"Pretty, ain't it?" he said in an exaggerated drawl, as if he were some backwoods drummer bent on a sale.

"None of them's hers," the man said, stepping away from the horses, into the open. He kept his feet apart in a belligerent stance.

"Mister, you seem to be doing all the talking. Is the lady deaf and dumb?"

The man brought his hands back, brushing the duster away from his pistol grips. He wore two guns, like some drugstore cowboy. He bent slightly into a menacing crouch.

"You take your jewelry and ride on," the man said. "The lady ain't interested."

"Here, you take it," Zak said, and tossed the necklace into the air. It made a high arc, and the man reached up to grab it.

Zak climbed down from his saddle just as the man caught the necklace. He stood facing the man.

"Think you're pretty smart, don't you?" the man said.

Zak said nothing. He stood straight and level-eyed, staring at the man.

"I think that necklace belongs to the lady," Zak said.

"I think you're full of shit, mister."

The man dropped the necklace onto the ground. His hands hovered like a pair of hunting hawks above his pistols, a pair of converted Navy Colts.

"You'll want to think about drawing those pistols," Zak said, making no move toward his own, a Walker Colt converted from percussion to centerfire.

"Why is that?"

"Because," Zak said, "I'm the quicksand under your feet."

The man's eyes widened, then flashed with anger. His hands dove for his pistols.

Zak's right hand streaked down toward his own holster.

The man's hands grasped the butts of his pistols. He started to draw them from their holsters. He seemed fast.

An eternity winked by in a single split second and Zak's Walker cleared leather. A *snick-click* as he hammered back, the sound cracking the silence like the first rattle of a diamondback's tail.

Zak held his breath, squeezed the trigger. The Colt bucked in his hand as it exploded with orange flame, belching out golden fireflies of burnt powder and a .44 caliber lead slug that slammed into the man's chest just as the muzzles of his pistols slid free of their holsters.

A crimson flower blossomed on the man's chest. His breastbone made a crunching sound as the ball smashed into it like a thousand-pound pile driver.

He dropped to his knees. His hands went slack and the pistols slid from his grasp and hit the ground. He opened his mouth to speak, and blood enough to fill a goblet gushed from his mouth.

He never took another breath and pitched forward, dead weight succumbing to gravity.

The woman let out a short cry.

A thin tendril of gray smoke spooled from the barrel of Zak's gun, scrawling in graceful arabesques before the wind shredded it to pieces that vanished like some sleight-of-hand illusion.

Zak reached down and picked up the necklace, held it up so the woman could see it.

"This yours?" he said, his voice as soft as kid leather.

The woman's eyes rolled back in their sockets and she slumped down on the seat in a sudden swoon.

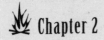 Chapter 2

Zak holstered his pistol, climbed up onto the seat of the old Concord. The woman lay on her back, her eyes closed, her face drained of color, a grayish tint around her lips. She was a beautiful young woman, with coal black hair, a patrician nose, fine structure to her cheekbones and jaw. Her lips were full and lightly rouged, and her cheeks bore a faint tint of vermillion, just enough to enhance her smooth, unblemished skin.

Zak straddled her, took her chin in one hand. He leaned down and blew gently on her face, then placed his hands on her shoulders and shook her.

"Ma'am, ma'am," he said, his voice low, slightly husky.

Her eyelids fluttered, then opened, closed quickly again.

The sun splashed on her pale face. She wore no bonnet and a strand of hair drooped over her forehead like a brown tassel. She wasn't down deep, he decided. Just floating beneath the surface of wakefulness. Maybe afraid to free herself from the darkness. Afraid of what she might see, of what might happen to her if she opened her eyes and kept them open.

"Miss," he said. "You can come to, ma'am. I'm not going to hurt you."

Her eyelids quivered. It was almost like a little spasm, a trembling manifested only on that part of her anatomy. As if, somewhere down where she was, she wanted to swim up, step from the dark ocean into the blinding sun. He wasn't touching her, just straddling her, one knee on the floorboard for balance, the other leg pressing against the seat. He touched her face, smoothed his fingers down one cheek as if stroking her back to life in the gentlest way.

Her eyelids stopped quivering. Then they batted open and her blue eyes fixed on his face. He held up a hand to shield the sun from beaming down into her eyes. A shadow painted that part of her face.

"You got to wake up, ma'am," he said. "Might be time you told me what happened on this coach."

She closed her eyes, then quickly opened them again. Wider this time, as if she were alarmed, perhaps afraid. He eased away from her, scooted up on the far side of the seat. The sun struck her in the eyes and she winced, turned her head so the light no longer blinded her.

"Did you . . ."

"Did I what?"

"Kill that man. Jenkins."

"He played the card."

"Played the card?" She put one hand on the seat and pulled herself into a sitting position on the floorboards. She pulled the strand of hair away from her face, tucked it away in the folds of her hair.

"He called it. Opened the ball."

"You mean he . . ."

"It's not hard to figure out. You saw him. He had two pistols he wanted to draw on me pretty bad. It could have been me down there on the ground."

"He's dead? Jenkins?"

"Yes. If you mean that man on the ground there. I didn't know his name."

"He was driving me to Fort Bowie when we were attacked by some Apaches."

"Did you see the Apaches?"

"Yes. Of course. They were all painted. They were brutal."

"Did you see them scalp the two soldiers?"

"Yes. It was horrible. They—They cut their throats first."

"I've never known the Apaches to take scalps," he said. "Are you sure they were Apaches?"

"Mr. Jenkins said they were."

"When did he say this? When they attacked, or after they had left?"

"I—I don't recall. I think he said it when they rode up and he stopped the coach."

"Did you hear the Apaches speak?"

"Yes. A few words."

"Have you ever heard Apache speech before?"

She shook her head. "But, I did understand a word or two they said. They spoke Spanish, and I've heard Spanish before."

"Were these men Mexicans trying to look like Apaches?"

She wrinkled up her nose and squinted, as if

trying to think. "They might have been. I don't know. It all happened so fast. Or seemed to."

"How come you threw your baubles off the coach?"

He reached into his pocket, drew out the items of jewelry and handed them back to her. She put them in her lap as if reluctant to put them back on her person.

"I—I was afraid of Mr. Jenkins."

"How come? He do something to you?"

"I—well, I can't be sure, of course, but when those Apaches, or Mexicans, dragged Lieutenant Coberly and Sergeant Briggs out of the coach, Mr. Jenkins was just outside. Earl and Fred resisted, of course. Jenkins made a little move. I thought he was holding a knife under his duster and it looked like he jabbed it into Earl's side. Lieutenant Coberly, I mean. It happened so quick. The Apaches shoved Jenkins away, but it looked staged."

"What do you mean?" he asked.

"They, the Indians, weren't very mean to Jenkins. The way they shoved him aside didn't look mean at all. It was just a feeling I got. And, when they didn't kill him, or me, I began to suspect that Jenkins might have known those men with their painted faces."

"Anything else made you think that?"

"Jenkins kept telling me I had to tell the soldiers at the fort what happened. He kept saying, 'those damned Apaches,' over and over. As if he wanted me to bear witness to officials at the army post."

"Why are you going to Fort Bowie?" he asked.

"My brother arranged for me to teach there."

"You're a schoolmarm?"

"No," she said, "I'm a teacher. Music and English."

"And your brother?"

"He is posted to Fort Bowie. He's a captain in the army."

"Name?"

"Name?"

"His name," Zak said.

"Ted O'Hara. Theodore. I'm his sister. My name's Colleen."

"Can you drive this team?"

She shrank back as if terrified at such a thought.

"No. I couldn't. I wouldn't know what to do."

"Let me tie my horse to the back of the coach. I'll drive you there."

"You have business in Fort Bowie?"

"Maybe," he said. "Look, do you want to ride in the coach, or up here with me?"

She looked at him, as if trying to size him up more thoroughly before making up her mind.

"I think I'd prefer to stay up here," she said. "Why?"

"Because I'm going to pick up those dead soldiers and Jenkins there and take 'em to Fort Bowie. If you ride in the coach, I'll have to carry 'em up there with your baggage." He nodded toward the luggage rack behind him.

"Oh," she said.

Zak hopped down from the coach and tied Nox to the straps on the boot. He slipped his canteen from the saddle horn, walked to the spring, filled it. He drank, then refilled it to the brim. He stoppered it and carried it back to his horse, slung it by its strap to his saddle horn, then strolled over to Jenkins. He reached down and jerked the knife from its scabbard, examined it.

There was dried blood on the blade, the color of rust. That would explain the wound he had seen in the lieutenant's side. He shoved the knife back in its scabbard, then picked up the man's pistols and slid them back into their holsters. He lifted the body and carried it to the coach. Jenkins had started to stiffen and he stank from voiding himself. Zak set him down, opened the door, then slid Jenkins's body inside, on the floor, in a sitting position, and closed the door. Then he climbed back up on the seat, picked up the reins, pulled the brake off and turned the team. Colleen never said a word, but sat there tight-lipped and wan, holding onto the side of her seat as she swayed from side to side.

The wood of the floorboards creaked and leather squeaked under the strain and motion of the coach. The wheels spun out a spool of rosy orange dust in its wake, and the wheels clanked against rocks and small stones. The sky was a pale blue, with little white cloud puffs scattered like bolls of cotton across the vast ocean of blue. They hung nearly motionless in the still air, and nothing marred the view until they saw the buzzards circling above the place where the soldiers lay dead.

He saw Colleen cringe when they came to where the coach had been stopped and attacked. He swung the rig in a half circle and brought it to a stop a few yards from the two bodies of the soldiers. Buzzards hopped around the corpses, flapping their wings. Cody set the brake and climbed down.

He walked over to the bodies, and the buzzards lifted into the air, a half dozen of them, their pinions clawing for purchase to raise their ungainly bodies from the ground, make them airborne.

He picked up Lieutenant Coberly first, carried him to the coach. He lay him down by the door and went back for the sergeant. When he had them both there, he opened the door and placed each body inside, stacked them next to Jenkins in sitting positions. The bodies of the soldiers were stiff, their eyes plucked out, their ears and noses gouged of flesh from the beaks of the scavengers. He closed the door and walked back, studying the unshod pony tracks.

He followed the tracks for some distance, five hundred yards or so, until he was satisfied. The riders had headed off in the direction of Tucson. He couldn't be sure, of course, but it would be unlike any Apache to ride to a white man's town after killing two soldiers. When he returned to the coach, where Colleen was waiting, looking straight ahead and not at him, he climbed back up onto the seat, released the brake.

"Had the . . . had the buzzards . . ." Her voice trailed off.

"You don't want to think about that," he said.

He rippled the reins across the backs of the horses and they stepped out.

She didn't speak to him again until after they had passed Apache Springs.

"You know who I am," she said. "You know my name."

He said nothing.

"I don't know yours."

"No."

"Do you mind telling me who you are? What is your name?"

"Cody."

"Just Cody?"

"Zak Cody."

"Zachary?"

"No, just Zak."

She spelled it: "Z-A-C-H?"

"No. Z-A-K. My father couldn't spell too well."

"Cody," she said. "I've heard that name before. Somewhere. From my brother Ted, I think. Do you know him?"

"No, I don't."

"That's odd. I'm sure he's mentioned you. It'll come to me in a minute."

"It's not important," he said.

"It is to me."

"Why?"

"It might tell me who you really are. You don't talk much."

"When I have something to say, I talk."

"You're not in the army."

"No."

"But you were."

"I was."

"Ah, that's at least something."

"Is it?"

"Why, yes. It explains why you're going to Fort Bowie."

"Does it?"

"Well, I would think so."

Cody said nothing. A cloud passed below the sun, throwing a shadow over the trail. They both listened to the creak and clank of the coach as it rumbled through rough, rocky country that was almost flat and seemingly endless, with only cactus and mesquite to break the monotony.

Cody did not know why Colleen's brother might have mentioned his name, and it wasn't important. But if Ted O'Hara knew who he was, then some of his past might come out and he couldn't help that. A man carried his past with him. It followed him like a shadow.

"General Crook," she said.

"What?" Cody said.

"Were you with General Crook?"

"Yes, I was."

"I remember now. Ted said you saved Crook's life once. Is that true?"

Cody shrugged. "Who knows about such things?" he said. "I won't claim credit for such."

But she looked at him with different eyes now, as she recalled what her brother had said once, when speaking with other officers. Zak Cody, she decided, was no ordinary man. From the tone of Ted's voice, from the obvious respect and admiration implied by what he'd said, Zak Cody was almost a legend. But that was all she knew about him.

And, she wanted to know more.

Much more.

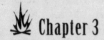 Chapter 3

Colonel Crook did not see the Paiutes. The red man rose up off the ground, his naked body covered with earth, and crept up behind him, a war club raised over his head ready to brain the officer. Zak appeared out of nowhere, just as Crook turned and saw the Paiute. Silent as a wraith, Zak grabbed the Indian by the hair, pulled his head back and sliced his neck open with a knife, letting the lifeblood flow until the Indian went limp in his arms, his chest and legs shining red with blood. The kill was quick and merciless, and Crook felt a shiver course up his spine.

The memory of that day had come unbidden, dredged up by Colleen. Zak shook it off, but he knew it would come back. It always did.

He knew she was looking at him, trying to figure him out, perhaps trying to remember all that her brother had said about him. That's the way people were. They all wanted to know your past, as if that was the key to knowing who a man was now. He was not the same man who had fought alongside Crook in his battle with the Paiutes. A lot of water had gone under the bridge since then. But he also knew he was forever bound to General George Crook, as Crook was bound to him.

Over the beige land they rode with their grisly cargo. Low hills, studded with rocks and cactus, appeared on their flanks, looking like ancient ruins, rubble from once majestic cities that rose above the land, then crumbled to dirt and broken stone.

Zak stopped the coach at Apache Springs.

"You might want to drink," he said. "I'm going to water the horses. This is the only water hereabouts."

"Yes," she said. "I am thirsty. And I want to stretch my legs."

He unhitched the horses, leading them one by one to the crystal clear stream to drink. The others, left behind, whickered in anticipation. Colleen cupped her hands, dipped them in the water where it emerged from the rocks, and slaked her thirst. Then she walked over to the oak trees that bordered the stream and took some shade beneath the leafy branches.

Hills rose up on both sides of the long basin that sequestered the sparkling spring. It was a peaceful place, an oasis in the harsh desert where yucca bloomed like miniature minarets. There was cholla, too, beautiful, delicate, and dangerous, prickly pear that the Mexicans called *nopal*, and there, too, grew stool and agave.

"What's that I hear?" Colleen said as Zak led Nox to the stream. "Over there, in the hills."

"Probably Fort Bowie," he said.

"We're that close and you stopped to water the horses?"

"Yes'm."

"We could have watered them at the fort."

"Yeah. Now we don't have to."

She walked over to him, stood in the glaring sun. "With those men in there, you stopped, took all this time."

"They're not going anywhere, ma'am."

"No, but they—they're . . ."

"I don't want a lot of chores to do when we get to the fort."

"Just what is your business at the fort?" There was a demanding tone in her voice.

"Personal."

"I hardly think an army post is the place to conduct personal business."

Nox finished drinking and Zak started walking back to the coach, leading the horse with the reins.

"Ma'am, out here, the army serves as the eyes and ears of the public. They generally know who comes and who goes."

"So, you're looking for someone."

"I'm going to ask about someone, yes."

"I don't think it's your place to use the army for your own personal agenda, Mr. Cody. But I expect they'll tell you that at Fort Bowie."

He hitched Nox to the coach. They could hear voices from the fort. They floated on the vagrant breezes, wafting here and there, fragments of loud conversations that made no sense. A Gambel's quail, sitting atop a yucca some distance from them, piped its call, as if serving notice of its presence to any who would hear. A Mexican jay answered the call with harsh *whenks* from its throat, scolding the quail with its plumed topknot.

"Yes'm," he said, without protest.

"You're a strange man, Zak Cody," she said. "I don't know what to make of you."

"Easy decision, then."

"What?"

"You don't have to make anything of me. I'm what I am. Accept it or reject it."

"Well, so you do have a mind after all," she said.

Zak said nothing. He drew a deep breath and looked around at the ruins of the old fort. There wasn't much left. Wind and rain and neglect had pretty much wiped out all traces of the original Fort Bowie. The desert took back everything that was left to it. That's one thing he liked about the desert. It treated civilization harshly. People passed through it at their own risk.

"What are you looking at?" she asked, following his gaze.

"The fort used to be here," he said. "Do you know the story?"

"No."

"There was a big fight here, back in 'sixty-two, during the War Between the States. Chiricahua Apaches and United States troops."

"I didn't know that. What happened?"

"It was July, and Captain Tom Roberts got ambushed here. Chiricahuas. He was coming from California to fight the Confederate invasion of New Mexico. He lined up his mountain howitzers and blasted the Apaches. Scared hell out of them."

"You were here?" she said.

Zak shook his head. "No, but I heard about it."

"I think we've wasted enough time here, Mr. Cody."

He helped her onto the coach, took his seat beside her. A few minutes later they reached the fort, beyond the pass. It lay in a saddle in the mountains, east of Apache Springs. There were a lot of buildings, some made of adobe, some of stone, others, frame dwellings, made from lumber. A steam pump pulled water from a well. A flagpole stood in the center of the ramada, its banners flapping in the breeze.

"So, this is Fort Bowie," Colleen said.

"This is the second Fort Bowie. Troops have only been here since 'sixty-nine, so it's still pretty new."

He pulled the coach up in front of the corrals and stables. A corporal came out to greet them.

"Howdy, ma'am," he said, "welcome to Fort Bowie." Then he looked at Zak.

"Where's the regular driver," the young man asked. "Jenkins?"

"He's in the coach," Zak said.

"What's he doin' in the coach?" The young man's face scrunched up in genuine puzzlement.

"Nothing," Zak said.

"Huh?"

The corporal walked over to the side door and opened it. He jumped back in surprise.

"Holy shit," he said.

"Mr. Cody," Colleen said, "will you escort me to meet the post commander?"

"Sure," Cody said. He spoke to the corporal. "That black horse, rub him down and grain him, will you, soldier?"

"Wh-What about what's in the coach? Those men are dead, ain't they?"

"Yes."

"Shit, I got to report this."

Zak walked back to his horse, slid the rifle from its scabbard and lifted his saddlebags from behind the cantle. He patted Nox's withers and walked back to the stunned soldier.

"Can you point out the post commander's office, son?"

"Over yonder. Where you see the flagpole. He ain't in, though. Major Willoughby's acting in his stead. I got to report what's in that coach."

"Do it, then," Zak said.

The corporal ran off toward the guard house, legs pumping, arms flying around in all angles. Zak slung his saddlebags over his shoulder, shifted his rifle to his left hand. He crooked his arm and Colleen slipped her arm in it and they walked toward the large building beyond the parade ground. Soldiers walked here and there, not even mildly curious. Flies buzzed around their heads and the hot sun beat down. The flags flapped on the flagpole, but the air was thick and hot and the breeze brought no cool with it.

A pair of mourning doves whistled overhead, twisting and turning in the air like feathered darts. The sound of a blacksmith's hammer ringing on iron wafted across the compound. The horses hitched to the coach whickered and swatted at flies with their tails. Two soldiers crossed in front of them. Both looked longingly at Colleen, who returned their smiles and gripped Zak's arm even tighter.

Two men stood guard at the entrance to the headquarters building. Both wore sergeant's stripes.

"Miss Colleen O'Hara to see Major Willoughby," Zak said.

"She can go in," one of the men said. "You'll have to show me some papers, sir."

Zak drew out a leather wallet from his pocket, handed it, open, to the sergeant.

"Yes, sir," the man snapped, with a salute. He handed the wallet back to Zak.

They entered the building, where more men stood guard, and walked to one seated at a desk.

"What was that all about, Mr. Cody?" Colleen whispered.

"My identification."

"And you rate a salute? A civilian?"

Zak said nothing.

"Major Willoughby," Colleen said to the clerk. "I'm Colleen O'Hara and this is Mr. Zak Cody."

"Yes'm," the corporal said. "Just one minute."

He left his desk, opened one half of a double door and went inside. A moment later he returned.

"You can go right in," he said. His gaze lingered on Cody for a long moment. Colleen noticed it and frowned.

"Who are you?" she whispered.

"Just who I said I am, Miss O'Hara."

Major Willoughby was a short, fastidious man, who rose up from behind a desk so neat and polished there was but a single paper atop it. There was a map of the territory on the wall behind the desk and a window that sparkled with sunlight, giving a view of the hills and part of the compound. The desk was flanked by an American flag and one bearing the insignia of the Second Cavalry. A man stood in a far corner, his back turned to the room.

"May I see your papers, Mr. Cody?" Willoughby

said. "And good afternoon to you, Miss O'Hara. We've been expecting you."

"Thank you, Major," she said.

"Please sit down," Willoughby said to her as he took Zak's wallet and opened it. Zak stood there, looking at the man whose back was turned to him.

"You've got some pay here at the post, Colonel," Willoughby said. "I think Lieutenant John Welch is the paymaster this month. Check with the quartermaster."

"I've got two of your men outside in the coach," Zak said. "They were with Miss O'Hara."

"That would be Sergeant Briggs and Lieutenant Coberly," the major said. "They were her escorts from Tucson. I wonder why they didn't report with you, Colonel."

"Because they're both dead," Colleen said. She shot an odd look at Cody. "Mr. Cody killed the driver, a man named Jenkins."

"What happened?" Willoughby's face had drained of color. It looked as if he'd swallowed a jar of paste and it had oozed out through his pores.

Colleen looked at Zak, but he said nothing.

"We—We were attacked," she said. "I think by Apaches. But Mr. Cody doesn't think they were Apaches."

"Why did you kill Jenkins?" the major asked.

"Because he was going to kill me," Zak said "Those soldiers were scalped, sir. I don't think Apaches take scalps."

The man in the corner turned around.

"You're right, Cody. They don't. Cochise doesn't

anyway, and he's the main thorn in our sides at the moment."

"Colonel Cody," Willoughby said, "shake hands with Tom Jeffords. He's the authority on Apaches in this neck of the woods."

The two men shook hands.

"I've heard of you, Jeffords," Zak said. "General Crook thinks very highly of you."

"I've heard of you, too, Cody, and the same holds for what Crook thinks of you."

"I'd like to see my brother now," Colleen said.

Willoughby froze. His eyes turned to flint.

Jeffords looked at Colleen, his face softening with an expression of concern. "I'm afraid that's not possible, Miss O'Hara," Jeffords said. "That's why I'm here with Major Willoughby. Your brother is missing."

Zak caught her on the way down as Colleen fell into a deep swoon, her legs collapsing beneath her.

"Damn," Willoughby said, his voice a raspy whisper. "If it weren't for the bad news, we wouldn't have any news at all out here."

Zak carried Colleen to a chair, looked at Willoughby.

"I'll get some water," Jeffords said, and left the room.

"Major," Zak said. "Don't call me Colonel. I'm not in the army anymore. You better read those papers in my wallet more carefully."

"But you carry the rank."

"Compliments of President Grant and General Crook, sir. But to you, I'm just an ordinary civilian."

Willoughby gulped and began to read the papers while Zak fanned Colleen's face. It was the second time she had fainted that day. He wondered that the woman could still go on, and how much more she could take before she'd have to be put in the post infirmary.

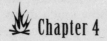 **Chapter 4**

Major Willoughby read the short note attached to the back of Zak's identity card, which listed him as Colonel Zak Cody, U.S. Army, retired.

To Whom It May Concern:

Colonel Zak Cody is hereby detached from the U.S. Army, insofar as his military duties are concerned. He is hereby attached to my office and is under my direct command and the command of General George Crook. He is to be given every courtesy by the U.S. Military. His connection to the President and to General Crook are considered Top Secret and shall not be revealed to any civilian or military personnel who do not need to know his rank and special assignments. Any breach of confidence regarding Colonel Cody shall be dealt with severely, and any military person who divulges the content of this letter will be subject to court-martial.

The letterhead bore the seal of the President of the United States and was signed by Ulysses S. Grant.

Willoughby walked around his desk and handed the wallet to Zak.

"I understand, sir. I'm sorry."

"That's all right, Major. You didn't know. Now you do."

"There are stories about you, you know."

"I know. I ignore them. You should do the same."

"Yes, sir," Willoughby said.

Jeffords returned with a glass of water and a pitcher. He set the pitcher on the desk and handed Zak the water. Together, he and Zak propped Colleen up in the chair. Zak held the glass to her lips and poured a small amount into her mouth.

She swallowed and her eyelids batted twice. She choked on a few drops, spluttered and opened her eyes wide. Sitting up straight, she reached out for Zak. It was a reflexive motion, much like a drowning person deploys toward a rescuer. Her fingers squeezed Zak's arms as she gulped in air.

"I—I'm sorry," she said. "I—I must have fainted."

She saw Jeffords kneeling there before her and her gaze locked on his.

"My brother. Ted. You said . . ."

"He's missing, Miss O'Hara. I'm sorry. I just found out this morning. I came here to report this to Major Willoughby."

"How? Why?"

Jeffords stood up and stepped aside. He gestured to Willoughby, who cleared his throat and walked over to stand in front of her.

"Ted rode out with a patrol early yesterday morning," Willoughby said. "We had reason to believe some Apaches were banding together on the San Simon. The patrol encountered no hostiles, but last night, apparently, your brother turned up missing. Tom ran into the patrol early this morning. They were tracking a small band of Apaches."

"They think Ted was grabbed during the night," Jeffords said. "We don't know why. They took his horse, too, so we know he's still alive."

"The patrol is still out?" Zak asked.

Willoughby nodded.

"They must find him," Colleen said. "Do you think they will, Mr. Jeffords?"

"There's a chance," he said.

Colleen opened her mouth to say something, but decided against it.

Just then a young lieutenant knocked on the door.

"Enter," Willoughby said.

"Sir, you'd better take a look at what we've got out there. It's pretty grim."

"All right, Neighbors. I'll be right there."

"It's in front of the livery, sir."

The young man saluted and left the room.

"Can I stay in Ted's quarters?" Colleen asked.

"No, it's not private," Willoughby said. "We have a billet for you, though."

"I'd at least like to see Ted's room. And my carpetbag's still inside the coach. My suitcase is on top."

"We'll see that you're accommodated, Miss O'Hara. Just let me sort all this out."

"You're right. You have more important things to worry about right now. I'll go with you and get my things."

"I'll see to it that you're shown to your quarters and someone carries your luggage for you." Willoughby swept past her. Jeffords followed. Zak took her arm and led her outside.

A crowd had gathered in front of the livery. All four coach doors stood wide open. Zak was surprised to see several white women in the crowd. The women all turned to look at Colleen, and some of them smiled at her.

Willoughby and Jeffords looked inside the coach. When the major finished his inspection, his complexion had turned ashen. He looked as if he had been kicked in the stomach. Jeffords took longer. When he turned around, he looked at Zak, shook his head.

"You might want to introduce yourself to the women, Colleen," Zak said. "I'll get your carpetbag and suitcase for you."

"Thank you," she said.

Zak walked over to Jeffords.

"Those men weren't scalped by Apaches," Tom said.

"No. I didn't figure such."

"Let's have a talk, Cody. I know you've got business with Major Willoughby you haven't even mentioned yet, but I want to fill you in on some things."

The two men walked over to the stables, stepped inside where it was cool. Willoughby was issuing orders to the post surgeon and assigning men to burial detail. It was plain to Zak that Willoughby was rattled by what he had seen. Obviously, there was a reason he'd been left in charge of the post. He was probably good at organization, but did not

handle himself well under fire. It was something
Zak noted when dealing with people, and it often
gave him an advantage over men he did not per-
sonally know well.

Nox was tied up at the far end of the stables,
his bridle replaced by a rope halter. He chomped
on corn and oats set before him in a small trough.
Other horses stood looking out of stalls, or rubbed
up against the walls and posts. There was the sound
of switching tails and low whickers as others fed
or drank. Flies buzzed in an insistent monotonous
drone. The smell of urine and manure, thick and
pungent, mixed with the musty scent of straw.

Jeffords slid his hat toward the back of his head,
cocking the brim up to show his face, the salt and
pepper sideburns. He was a lean, wiry man, with
weathered lines in his face, clear blue eyes set wide
on either side of his chiseled nose.

"Cody, I'll be straight with you. I'm probably the
only one on this post who will. There's a whole lot
of war going on in this part of Arizona, and it's not
just with the Apaches."

"What are you driving at, Jeffords?"

"That business with the coach, for one. Those
soldiers weren't scalped by any Apache."

"I figured that."

"The whites around here want the Apaches
wiped out, shipped out, buried, gone. I think this
latest incident proves that the situation is coming
to a head."

"The army know this?"

"It does and it doesn't. The army is dealing with
some marauding Apaches. But the Apaches are
being goaded, too, by whites who want the army

chasing them clear out of the territory. I'm trying to make peace, but right now it looks pretty hopeless. The Apaches don't know one white man from another, and right now they think the whole world is against them."

"You have a line on who attacked the coach?" Zak asked.

"Your guess is as good as mine, but the owner of the line, Ferguson, is in this up to his armpits. And the word is that he and other businessmen have hired some outside help."

The hackles bristled on the back of Cody's neck.

"Outside help? Maybe from Taos?"

Jeffords's eyebrows arched. His eyes widened in surprise.

"There was some talk about Ferguson bringing in a gang of hired guns from Taos. I was trying to get a line on that news when I got word about Ted O'Hara being sent out on patrol. By that damned Willoughby. That was against my recommendation and directly against Captain Bernard's specific orders."

"Bernard. Reuben Bernard? Isn't he the commanding officer of Fort Bowie?"

"Yeah, he is. Then some idiot sent Major Willoughby down here and put him in charge. Reuben is putting out fires all over the territory, chasing Apaches with a vengeance, attacking their villages, burning their homes. It's an ugly situation. I can't prove it, but someone leaked information about Ted O'Hara, who never should have left this post with a damned patrol."

"Why?"

"Ted has been working with me, under orders

from high up, Crook, in fact. He has information about Cochise and other Apache leaders I've been talking to. It's not just chance that he was picked out from that night camp and taken hostage. Someone wants the information he has in that Irish head of his."

"Will O'Hara tell what he knows?"

"Not unless he's tortured beyond endurance. And even then, I think he'd die before he divulged what he knows. He's trying as much as I to bring the Apaches to the peace tent."

"What exactly does O'Hara know?" Zak asked.

"He knows where all the secret camps of the Apache are. He's been to them. With me."

"Did Willoughby know this when he sent O'Hara out on patrol?"

"I think so. He had to know."

"So, do you think Willoughby deliberately sent O'Hara out so that he could be kidnapped?"

There was a silence between the two men. Jeffords squared his hat again. He looked off toward the horseless coach and let out a deep expulsion of breath.

"I hate to think that," he said. "But Willoughby, on his way out here from Tucson, spent time in Vail and Tucson, meeting with the townspeople. They could have gotten to him, persuaded him toward their point of view."

"And what is that?" Zak asked.

"That the Apaches do not want peace and that they can't be trusted. That the U.S. Army should wipe them out like they would a bunch of rattlesnakes. Bernard holds to that view as well, I fear."

"Have you heard talk of a man named Ben Trask?" Zak said.

"Trask. From Taos?"

"Yeah."

"Wait a minute. There was a man killed in Taos, in 'sixty-nine, I think. His name was Cody. Related?"

"My father. Russell Cody. Trask murdered him. And it was 'sixty-eight. I've been tracking him for a good three years."

"Cochise spoke of this man," Jeffords said.

"He did? When?"

"At least a year ago. Cochise's band was accused of wiping out several families, murdering them, burning down their houses. Cochise said a man named Trask was responsible."

"So, Trask has been out here for some time."

"You might learn more in Tucson, or Vail. Cochise tracked him to those two towns after coming across those depredations he was accused of."

Zak's mind filled with thoughts of his father and how he had died at the hand of Ben Trask. Russell Cody had come to Taos to live out his remaining years. When the beaver gave out and the fur trade collapsed, he took his money and bought a ranch in South Dakota, raised cattle and wheat. He drove cattle up from Texas, sold them for good prices, saved his profits. He sold his ranch, moved to Taos, and made even more money as a trader, selling silver in the East and hauling back goods to sell in Santa Fe and Taos.

Cody's father had been trading for gold, as well. He had not trusted the banks, so kept his hoard hidden. Trask had tortured Russell to learn the hiding place, then, after getting the gold, he killed Russell in a most brutal way, mutilating his body, leaving him for the wolves, the coyotes, and the buzzards. Zak envisioned a similar fate for Ted O'Hara if Trask was behind his kidnapping.

"So, I guess I can't trust Willoughby," Zak said.

"If I were you, Cody, I wouldn't trust anybody on this post. Or anywhere else, for that matter."

"Thanks, Tom. You've been a big help to me."

"What are you going to do, Cody? You can't go after these men all alone. They're dead serious and determined to achieve their goals at any cost."

"Desperate men make mistakes," Zak said. "I'll ride to Tucson, see what I can find out. If nothing, I'll go to Vail."

"Dangerous places for someone seeking information about the men behind this scheme to wipe out the Apache."

"Then that's where I have to go. What about you?"

"Right now I'm the only white man who can talk with the Apaches, try to bring peace to this region. I'll talk to that patrol when they come in, see what I can find out about Ted's disappearance."

"If I find out anything, I'll get word to you, here at Bowie."

"Fair enough."

The two men shook hands and walked back to the coach. Willoughby had been staring at them, a scowl on his face. He turned away when they both looked at him.

Zak walked over to Colleen, who had been talking to some of the women.

"I'm going to try and find your brother, Colleen. Just don't tell anyone about it."

"Why?"

"Maybe I'll tell you someday. You take care. Hold on to hope."

"Do you know where Ted is?"

"I'm going to find out. Take care."

He turned and walked up to a soldier.

"Can you direct me to the paymaster's office?" Zak asked.

The soldier pointed to a building.

A half hour later Zak rode out of Fort Bowie, into the setting sun. He felt a great weight lift from his shoulders. He was glad to be away from Willoughby.

But he kept a wary eye on his backtrail, and he bypassed Apache Springs. He took to open country and felt right at home.

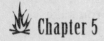 Chapter 5

The tracks were still fresh, clearly visible even in the hazy light of dusk, when Zak's shadow stretched long across the land. It was a place to start. Perhaps this trail would lead him to where he wanted to go, and perhaps it would cross other trails of interest to him.

The clouds in the western sky, long thin loaves, were bronzed, and rays of gossamer light shone like sprayed columns from beneath the horizon. A roadrunner dashed across the unshod pony tracks, legs working like high-speed darning needles. It disappeared among red and golden rocks that were turning to ash on the eastern side. Zak followed the tracks on a northwesterly course, studying them as he rode, wondering about the riders until, after a mile or two, he determined that his hunch had been correct. They were not Apaches.

He found cigarette stubs tossed to one side, barely visible in the fading light. These were hand-rolled. Later, he reined up when he spotted a crumpled piece of paper on the ground. He dismounted, picked it up, and smoothed it out. It was a label from a package of pipe tobacco. The name stamped on the paper was PIEDMONT PIPE TOBACCO.

"Careless," he said to himself. "Or sloppy." He tucked the paper into his pocket and climbed back into the saddle. He did not know who he was following, but he knew damned well the riders were not Apaches.

When it grew too dark to see clearly, he began looking for a place to throw down his bedroll and spend the night. He found a spot partially hidden by stool, chaparral, mesquite, and yucca, rimmed by prickly pear. There was grain in his saddlebags for Nox, and he would chew on jerky and hardtack and make no fire.

He dismounted, hobbled Nox, fed him half a hatful of grain. As he walked around, his spurs went *jing jing,* and he took them off, preserving the silence of evening, allowing him to hear any sounds foreign to that place. He ate and watched the sky turn to ash in the west, felt the cool breeze on his face, sniffed the aroma of the desert's faint perfume as if it were a living, breathing thing that sighed like a pleasured woman.

It was full dark when Zak lay down on his bedroll, unholstered pistol by his side, within easy reach. Bats plied the air, scooping up flying insects, their wings whispering as they passed overhead. A multitude of stars glistened and winked like the lights of a distant town, their sparkles made more brilliant by the inky backdrop of deep space. The moon had not yet risen when he closed his eyes and thought about his father and how he had met his gruesome death.

Ben Trask had used a fireplace poker to burn Russell's flesh. He had stripped off his prisoner's shirt and pants, applied the red hot iron to his arms and chest. Then he had touched the poker to his father's testicles, as his men looked on and laughed at Russell's screams. When he had found out what he wanted to know, Trask made sure that Russell died a slow death.

He cut open his belly with a surgeon's precision until his father's intestines spilled out in blue-gray coils. Trask and his men had watched his father die, heard him beg for a bullet to his brain. They watched the elder Cody die slowly, his great strength drained from him, his tortured breathing descending to a rasp in his throat before it turned into a final death rattle.

Zak knew all this because a Mexican boy, Jorge Vargas, living next door, had watched it all through his father's window, powerless to help, his family gone to market that morning when the men rode up and entered Russell's adobe home.

From Jorge's description, he knew the man who had killed his father. Their paths had crossed before, in a Pueblo cantina when he and his father had come down from the mountains, following Fountain Creek. Ben Trask had a reputation even then. A hardcase. A gunny who preyed on prospectors and miners, a merciless killer without a trace of conscience.

All in the past, he thought, and no more grieving for his father. Instead, a vow he had made when he found his father's body and learned the story of his death. If there was such a thing as justice in the

world, then Russell's death demanded it. An eye
for an eye. A life for a life.

Zak folded into sleep, descended to that great
ocean of dream where the events of the day were
transformed into an odd journey through bewil-
dering mazes inside massive canyons, where guns
turned into unworkable mechanisms and people's
faces were ever-shifting masks that concealed their
true identities, and horses galloped across dream-
scapes like shadowy wraiths and every shining
stream turned to quicksand beneath the dreamer's
awkward and clumsy feet.

It turned cold during the night, and Zak had to
pull the wool blanket over him. He awoke before
dawn, built a quick fire and boiled coffee. He never
looked at the flames and stayed well away from the
glow, scanning the horizon, listening for any alien
sound. He relieved himself some distance away in a
small gully and covered up his sign. He was sipping
coffee as a rent appeared in the eastern sky, pouring
cream over the horizon until the land glowed with
a soft peach light that grew rosy by the time he
had finished and put on his spurs. He checked his
single cinch and gave Nox a few handfuls of grain,
then let him drink water from his canteen, which
he poured into his cupped left hand. He checked
his rifle and pistol, rolled up his bed and secured
it inside his slicker behind the cantle. He did not
eat, a habit he had formed long ago. When he went
hunting, it was always on an empty stomach.

Gently rolling country now, bleak, desolate, quiet,
as the sun rose above the horizon, casting the earth
and its rocks and flora into stark relief. The rocks

seemed to glow with pulsating color, and the green leaves of the yucca, the pale blossoms, took on a vibrancy that Zak could almost feel. It was the best time of day in the desert, still cool, yet warm with the promise of diurnal life returning to a gray black hulk of territory glazed pewter by the moon, now only a pale ghost in a sky turning blue as cobalt.

He rode over a rise, following the pony tracks, and there it was, nestled in the crotch of a long wide gully that fell away, then rose again several hundred yards from its beginning. An old adobe hut, still in shadow, stood on a high hump of ground, nestled against a flimsy jacal that joined it on one crumbling side. A mesquite pole corral bristled on a flat table some two hundred yards away. Zak counted eight horses in the corral, some with noses buried in a rusty trough, another one or two drinking out of half a fifty-gallon drum, next to a pump outside the corral.

Six of the horses were small, unshod, pinto ponies, actually, while the remaining two were at least fifteen hands high and were shod. They were rangy animals, looked as if they hadn't seen a curry comb or brush, and he could almost count their ribs. None of the horses looked up at him, and Nox didn't acknowledge them with a welcome whinny, either.

A thin scrawl of smoke rose from the rusted tin chimney set in the adobe part of the dwelling. It hung in the motionless air below the gully's rim. It appeared to be coming from an untended fire, possibly one that had been banked the night before. There was no sign of life in either the adobe or the jacal, but Zak knew someone had to be inside. He debated with himself for a moment whether to ride up to the door or walk up and hail the occupant.

It took him only a moment to decide. A man on foot was not of much use in such country. Whoever lived there could be off at a well or hunting jackrabbits for all he knew, and could return at any moment. If he was off his horse, he would be caught flat-footed and might lose Nox. There could be a number of men inside the hut, and more out roaming around.

He rode up to the door without being challenged.

He loosened the Walker Colt in its holster, slid the Henry rifle out of its scabbard a half inch.

"Hello the house," Zak called.

He waited, listening.

Nox's ears stiffened and fixed on the door as they both heard sounds from inside. The sun cleared the lower rim of the gully and shone on the sod roof of the adobe like spilled liquid gold.

"*Quien es?*" a voice called out.

"*Un viajero,*" Zak replied. "*Quiero comprar un caballo.*"

There was a series of shuffling noises from inside the adobe. Then he heard the sound of a latch bar scraping against wood. A moment later the door swung open on creaky leather hinges. An unshaven, unkempt man wearing dirty baggy trousers, huarache sandals, suspenders over a grimy white undershirt, stood in the doorway, his brown eyes blinking in the glare of the sun. He wore a pistol on a worn ammunition belt. The pistol was a Navy Colt converted from cap and ball to percussion. The bullets looked to be .36 caliber. Deadly enough, Zak thought. He wore his holster low, just above his right knee.

"*Caballo? Tu quieres comprar un caballo? Tienes dinero?*"

"I have money," Zak replied in English, "in my pocket. *Habla ingles?*"

"Yes, I speak English. You are a traveler, you say. Where are you going? You do not look like you need a horse. You are sitting on a fine one."

"I need a packhorse. Maybe one of those ponies you have out there in the corral."

The man's eyes shifted in their sockets. "Ah, the pony, eh? You would buy a pony to use for a pack-horse?"

"I'm a prospector," Zak lied. "I need to carry some ore to Tucson. That is where I am going."

"Ah, to Tucson? To the assay office? You have found gold?"

"I do not know what I have found."

"Where did you find this?"

Zak cocked a thumb and gestured over his shoulder. The man looked off in that direction, a look of disbelief on his face.

"There is no gold there," the man said, and took a half step backward. His face fell back into shadow. "There is an army fort. Maybe you can buy a horse there. I do not wish to sell the ponies."

"Mister, you step outside where I can see you, or I'll blow your head off as sure as you're standing there."

The Mexican hesitated. His right hand sank toward the butt of his pistol. It hovered there like a frozen bird with its wings spread for a long moment.

"You would draw the pistol on me?" he asked.

"If you don't step out right now. I'll draw so fast you won't even see it."

The man laughed and raised his arms, wiggled them to show that he wasn't going to draw his pistol. He stepped down from the doorway and stood there, looking up at Zak.

"You mean to rob me, then? I have nothing. I am a poor man with only those few horses you see out there."

"Just don't move," Zak said, and swung down from the saddle. He let the reins trail as he walked up close to the man. "What do you call yourself?" he asked.

"I am called Felipe. Felipe Lopez. You will not shoot me, eh?"

"I ask the questions, Felipe."

"Ask me anything. Just do not shoot me. Take the pony. There is no need to kill me over a horse."

"I want to know who those men were. They were riding those ponies yesterday."

"Men? What men? I do not know what you are talking about."

"Don't lie to me, Felipe, or you'll hear a rattle."

"A rattle?"

"Yeah, a rattle. That'll be the rattlesnake you stepped on, and that would be me. That's all you'll hear before I blow your lamp out. I want to know who those men were, who they work for and where they went."

Felipe said nothing for several seconds, as if he were weighing his chances, or trying to think up a good lie for the gringo.

"There were some men," he said. "They rode up

here and traded those ponies for six of my good horses. My best horses. They were outlaws, I think. They did not pay me. They rode off. I do not know where they went."

Zak knew the man was lying. He thought he was a pretty good liar. Likely, he'd had a lot of practice.

"That was a good story, Felipe. You ought to thank me."

"Thank you? Why?"

"For letting you stay alive a few more minutes. Now, maybe you can live even longer by telling me the truth."

"That is the truth. I swear it on my mother's honor."

"I doubt your mother has any honor, Felipe. I heard she was a whore."

Felipe's eyes narrowed to slits. The skin of his face stretched taut as his lips compressed, his teeth clenched.

"*Ten cuidado*," Felipe said, his voice a gruff whisper.

Zak looked straight into the man's flashing brown eyes.

"Be careful," Felipe had said in Spanish. And Felipe's body tensed into a coiled spring. He was like a tiger ready to pounce, Zak knew. Like a tiger cornered. He was a man without an ounce of fear. His mother's name had been besmirched by a gringo. There were few insults more scathing than calling a man's mother a whore.

Felipe was ready to fight.

To defend his mother's honor, dubious as that honor might be, Felipe was ready to die.

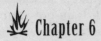 Chapter 6

Zak knew how dangerous Felipe had become. He'd just been slapped in the face with an insult so foul and demeaning that it had cut through to the core of the man's being. Few things were more sacred to a man than the woman who had given him life, his mother. Felipe was ready to put his life on the line in defense of the woman who had birthed him.

"All you have to do, Felipe," Zak said, "is tell me the truth and I'll take back what I said about your mother."

"It is too late for that," Felipe said.

"I'll find those men anyway. I do not need to know their names. I do not need you to tell me where they went. I will find them."

Felipe drew back, cocked his head and looked more closely at Zak.

"Who are you?" he said. "What do you call yourself?"

"Cody."

Felipe spewed air through his nostrils.

"Are you the one they call *Jinete de Sombra*?"

"I am sometimes called 'Shadow Rider.'"

"Because you wear the black clothes and ride the black horse."

"No," Zak said. "Because I am like a shadow. I come upon a man with no sound. I am not seen and I am not heard until it is too late."

"Ah, I wondered. You are the Indian fighter. You are the one who rode with the general they call Crook."

"I am the one."

"Then, perhaps you come here to kill Apaches, no?"

"Maybe," Zak said.

"Then you and I, we are on the same side. I, too, would kill Apaches. And the men you seek. They, too, wish all the Apaches killed. Maybe you would like to join them."

"Maybe."

"That is why you hunt them?"

"I wish to talk to them, yes."

"I think they would like to talk to you, Cody."

"Now we are getting somewhere, Felipe. I want to know who those men were who painted themselves like Apaches, rode the ponies here. I want to know who they work for."

"You ask much, Cody. But I will tell you so that you will go and leave me alone. Perhaps I will see you again one day."

"Perhaps."

"The men you look for have gone to Tucson. You must see a man named Ferguson. He owns the freight line."

"I am looking for a man named Ben Trask," Cody said.

"Ah, you know this man?"

"Yes, I know him."

"You are friends, no?"

Cody didn't answer. He let the question hang and watched Felipe squirm inside his skin. He could almost see the man's mind working, the way his forehead wrinkled up and his nose crinkled, making his eyes squint.

"This one, Trask, he is there. He works for Ferguson."

That was all Zak wanted to hear.

Trask was just the kind of man to stir up trouble with the Apaches, but he'd bet money that he had something else on his mind, as well. Trask might be working for Ferguson, but he was also working for himself, perhaps looking for an opportunity to make some illegal money.

"All right, Felipe. I'm leaving now."

"You do not want another horse?"

"No. You keep them."

Zak looked around at the ground, the maze of wagon tracks. The adobe with its adjoining jacal was some kind of way station, he was sure. Someone had to haul in fodder for the horses, food and supplies for Felipe. He wondered how many such stations were scattered over the territory. Someone had gone to a great amount of trouble to stir up hatred against the Apaches.

"What have you got inside that adobe?" Zak asked suddenly.

"Nothing."

"I want to take a look."

"No. This is not permitted."

"Are you hiding something in there?"

"No. I hide nothing."

"I think you are, Felipe. Step aside. I'm going to take a look."

Felipe hesitated. Zak took a step toward him, his right hand dropping to the butt of his pistol. It was a menacing move, deliberate, and Felipe got the message.

"Go inside, then."

"You first," Zak said.

Felipe shrugged. He turned and stepped inside, Cody right behind him. The hovel smelled of wood smoke and stale whiskey. A potbelly stove stood near the back wall, its fire gone out, but still leaking smoke from around its door and at a loose place on the pipe. A pot of coffee stood atop it, still steaming. Several bottles of whiskey lay on the floor, and half-empty bottles sat on a grimy table in the center of the room. The bunk in a corner reeked of sweat. On a sideboard he found several small cans of paint and brushes that had not yet been cleaned with the linseed oil standing nearby, next to a grimy wooden bowl.

Something caught Zak's eye in another corner. He walked over, his stomach swirling with a sensation like winged insects.

"What's this?" he said as Felipe stood there, his face waxen.

"I do not know. Those were there when I came here."

"Bullshit," Zak said as he picked up an army canteen. A blue officer's uniform lay in a heap. Silver lieutenant's bars gleamed from the shoulders of the tunic. A pair of cavalryman's boots, shiny, with a patina of dust on them, spurs still attached, stood against the wall behind the pile of clothes.

"I do not know who left those clothes," Felipe said.

"Do you know the name of the man who owns them?"

"No."

"Maybe you know Lieutenant Ted O'Hara."

"I do not know him," Felipe said.

Zak had seen enough. He was sure that Ted O'Hara had been brought to this place. They had stripped him of his uniform, put civilian clothes on him, perhaps. Then they had taken him someplace else. A hostage, maybe? A bargaining chip? Or maybe to torture him for information about the location of Apache camps, knowledge they somehow knew he possessed.

"You want some advice, Felipe?"

"What advice?"

"When I tell the army about this place, they're going to swarm all over you like a nest of hornets. If you're smart, you'll get on one of those horses out there and clear out."

"I have done nothing."

"I think you have. You're lucky I'm in a hurry or I'd pack you off to Fort Bowie trussed up like a Thanksgiving turkey."

Felipe, wisely, said nothing. He held his breath and walked outside with Zak.

"You leave now?" Felipe said.

"I might be back. In any case, someone will. You'd better find another place to hang your hat, Felipe."

Felipe stood in front of the door, speechless.

Zak knew his encounter with the man wasn't over. He had given Felipe fair warning. The next move was up to him. Felipe could either let him ride off or he could try to stop him.

Either way, the writing had already been painted on the wall.

Zak started to walk back to his horse when he heard a sound, the whisper of metal sliding out of leather. He knew what it was. Felipe was drawing his pistol.

Zak spun around, went into a fighting crouch. His right hand streaked to the butt of his Walker Colt. His gaze fixed on Felipe's eyes, not on his hand. But he could see, in the same range of vision, the barrel of Felipe's pistol clearing leather, the snout rising like the rigid black body of a striking snake.

The Walker Colt seemed to spring into Zak's hand. His thumb pressed down on the hammer, pushing it back into full cock as he leveled the barrel at the Mexican.

Felipe fired his pistol. Too soon. The bullet plowed a furrow at Zak's feet as he squeezed the trigger of the Walker.

He looked down a long dark tunnel as the pistol exploded, gushing flame and lead, bucking in his hand. At the end of the tunnel, Felipe, in stark relief, was hammering back for a second shot. Zak's .44 caliber ball of soft lead struck him just below his rib cage with the force of a sledgehammer. Dust flew from his shirt and a black hole appeared like a quick wink that filled suddenly with blood.

The hammered bullet drove Felipe off his moorings and he staggered backward, slamming into the wall of the adobe. A crimson flower blossomed on his chest, the smell of his half-digested supper spewing from his stomach. He gasped for air and slid down the wall, his fingers turning limp, the pistol drooping, then falling from his grasp. His eyes clouded over, the spark fading like a dying ember. The pupils turned frosty as blood pumped through the hole in his chest, ran down into his lap.

Zak stepped toward Felipe, his pistol at full cock for another shot, if needed.

He heard the death gurgle in the man's throat, but Felipe was still alive, hanging onto life with labored breaths.

Smoke spooled from the barrel of Zak's pistol as he knelt down in front of the Mexican. He lifted the pistol, the action scattering the smoke to shreds.

"I won't say adios to you, Felipe," Zak said, his voice a soft rasp, just above a whisper. "God isn't going with you on this journey. He's just going to watch you fall into a deep hole. The next sound you hear will be me. Walking over your grave, you sonofabitch."

Felipe stretched out a hand toward Zak's throat. He tried to sit up. Something broke loose inside him and he coughed up blood. His eyes glazed over with the frost of death as he gave one last gasp and fell back, his lifeless body slumped against the adobe wall. His sphincter muscle relaxed and he voided himself.

Zak stood up, walked away from the sudden stench. He ejected the empty hull in the Colt's cylinder and dug a cartridge from his gun belt. He slid it into the empty cylinder and spun it, then eased the hammer down to half-cock before sliding the pistol back in his holster.

He walked down to the corral and opened the gate.

"Heya, hiya," Zak yelled, waving his hat at the horses and ponies. They all dashed through the opening and galloped off down the gully and up the slope. They disappeared over the rim and a quiet settled over the empty corral.

Zak walked back to the adobe and went inside. He picked up the tunic with the lieutenant's bars, folded it tightly, went outside and stuffed it in his saddlebag. Then he went back inside, took a lamp from a hook over the potbellied stove and dashed coal oil on everything flammable within reach.

He stepped to the door, dug out a box of matches, struck one and tossed it onto the floor. The flame sputtered for a moment, then caught. The oil flared and tongues of flame began to lick the clothing and empty boxes, the chairs and table. It spread to the jacal as Zak mounted Nox and rode off, following one of the wagon tracks that was laced with shod hoof marks. The jacal blazed bright in the morning sun and he heard bottles of whiskey explode inside the adobe. Black smoke etched a charcoal scrawl on the horizon, rising ever higher in the still air.

The horse tracks led west, beside the faint wagon wheel ruts, and he followed them, putting Nox into a canter. The wagon tracks made it easy, and the horse tracks were only a day old, with no rain nor strong wind to erase them.

Killing a man was not easy. It was never easy.

There was always that dark tunnel, that unknown blackness, that he saw and wondered about. Conscience? He didn't know. He knew only that death was so final, there was no second chance for those who went up against his gun. And the killing of a man always weighed heavy on his heart or his mind or, perhaps, his soul. Life was such a fleeting, fragile, troublesome journey, but to cut that journey short, for whatever reason, gave a man pause, made him reflect on his own breath, his own heartbeat, his own blood pulsing in his veins.

Felipe hadn't seen it coming. He hadn't thought that far ahead. But Zak had seen it. He could always see it in a man's eyes, that inkling of mortality, that wonder, just before death blotted out everything, just before the tunnel closed in darkness and the light that had been a man one moment plunged into final darkness the next.

There was one question Zak had meant to ask Felipe, but the Mexican had pressed it, had made that fatal decision to draw his pistol. So the question had never been asked. Had never been answered.

The question would have been: "Do you know a man named Major Willoughby?"

Zak would have read the answer in Felipe's eyes, even if he had never replied. Then he would have known who betrayed Ted O'Hara, and who told Ben Trask where O'Hara was.

Deep down inside him, though, Zak thought he knew the answer to the unasked question.

One day he would find the answer, and the proof to go along with it.

It was only a question of time.

He just hoped he would find Lieutenant Theodore O'Hara alive.

But he would find him.

That, he knew.

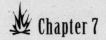 Chapter 7

Zak saw the flash out of the corner of his eye. It was bright as silver, as intense as a bolt of lightning. He had descended into a shallow depression and was just emerging when the dazzling light streaked from a low hill a half mile away. He kept on, but his gaze scanned the surrounding countryside.

That's when he saw an answering flash.

He knew he was not alone.

He built his first smoke of the day, casually taking out the papers and the pouch of tobacco. He rolled a quirly, licked it, stuck it in his mouth. He struck a match, drew smoke into his mouth and lungs. He knew he was being watched. His every move.

But who was watching?

The army?

He didn't think so. Troopers could be stealthy, but they'd had time to look him over and should have announced their presence long before he lit up a cigarette.

Apaches?

Likely. They probably had army signal mirrors, but they could use almost anything to reflect sunlight, send messages. A chunk of quartz, a piece of tin, broken glass from a bottle.

He looked at the ground, which had suddenly produced a maze of tracks. Besides the wagon ruts and horse tracks, the horses and ponies he had chased out of the mesquite pole corral had crossed his path. The tracks headed toward a point between the places where he had seen the flashing mirrors.

He had a decision to make.

He could follow his present course, toward Tucson, or shift to the new tracks.

Curiosity killed the cat, he thought.

He stayed to his tracking but could feel the watchers tracking him. It was an uncomfortable feeling, as if someone's eyes were boring into him, right between his shoulder blades. He saw no more flashes, but didn't expect any. The watchers knew where he was, and probably had a pretty good idea where he was going.

The land was gently rolling, swells of earth that rose up and fell away like an ocean frozen in motion. As long as the rises were shallow, he could still see ahead of him when he rode into a dip, but it was at the bottom of one of the depressions that he was brought up short.

They came in from two sides and made a line on the ridge above him. A dozen braves, Chiricahuas, he figured, all carrying rifles and wearing pistols. None were painted for war, but he knew that meant nothing. Apaches could go to war with or without decorating their bodies.

Zak's knowledge of Apache was limited. He had a smattering of Athabascan, knew a few words that amounted to very little if his life depended on much conversation. He could speak Spanish, though, and most of the Apaches had some familiarity with that language. Right now, he wondered if he would even have a chance to talk. The Indians surrounding him all had bandoleros slung over their shoulders, and the gun belts shone with brass cartridges.

He reined up, folded his hands atop one another on the saddle horn.

The Apaches looked at him for several moments.

If there was one trait that stood out among the Apaches, it was their patience. Zak figured he could match them on that score.

As he sat there, he heard the rumble of hoofbeats. More Apaches rode up, and they were driving the horses and ponies he had released from Felipe's corral. He turned and looked back at the smoke still rising in the sky.

One of the Apaches from the first bunch moved his pinto a few yards closer to where Zak sat his horse. His face was impassive, a bronze mask under straight black hair. He wore a red bandanna around his forehead, a faded blue chambray shirt, beaded white man's trousers, moccasins. He carried an old Sharps carbine that had lost most of its bluing. The stock was worn, devoid of its original finish. The pistol tucked into his sash was a cap and ball, a Remington, Zak figured, one of the New Model Army kind with a top strap.

The Apache spoke.

"*Quien eres?*" he said in Spanish.

"*Yo soy Cody.*"

"*Soldado?*"

"No, I'm not a soldier," Cody said, also in Spanish. Then he said, "*Nodeeh*," an Apache word, and touched his chest with his hand.

"*Nodeh ligai*," the Apache said. White man.

"Yes. Who are you?"

"*Anillo*," he said, and held up his left hand. Zak saw the ring on his finger, turquoise and silver. It sparkled in the sun.

"Ring," Zak said in English.

"Yes. I am called Ring. What do you do here?"

"I follow the tracks of bad white men. They made themselves to look like Apaches. They killed two soldiers."

"You gave us these horses?" Anillo said.

"Yes. I let them run from the corral."

"You burned the jacal and the adobe."

It was a statement, not a question. Zak nodded without speaking.

"Cody."

"Yes."

"The black horse is like a shadow."

"Yes. I call him *Noche*." He didn't figure Anillo would understand the Latin word for night.

"That is a good name. Cochise has spoken of you."

"I do not know Cochise. But I have heard he is a strong man. A brave man."

"He calls you *Jinete de Sombra*. Are you the Shadow Rider?"

"That is what some call me."

"Then we will not kill you, Cody."

"And I will not kill you. I make no fight with the Apache. I chase bad white men."

"Why do you do this?"

"General Crook does not like white men who cause

trouble with the Apache. He wants the Apache and the white men to live in peace."

Anillo spat upon the ground. His eyes narrowed and his face turned rigid with anger.

"Do you have tobacco?" Anillo asked.

"Yes."

"Then let us smoke and talk."

Zak reached in his pocket and pulled out the makings. Anillo spoke to one of the men in the group, gestured for him to come down. He dismounted. Zak slid from his saddle.

They sat down and the Apache who Anillo had called slid from his pony's back and walked over. He was older than Anillo. There were streaks of gray in his hair, lines in his face, wrinkles in the wattles under his chin. He had a fierce face, with close-set black eyes, a pug nose, high cheekbones burnished with the vermillion of his bloodlines.

"This is Tesoro," Anillo said. Then he spoke to Tesoro in Apache and the old warrior squatted down as Anillo took out a paper and poured tobacco into it. He handed the pouch and papers to Tesoro, who made himself a cigarette. He handed the makings to Zak, who rolled one for himself. The three sat together. The two Apaches leaned forward as Zak struck a match. He touched their cigarettes and they sucked smoke into their mouths. Zak lit his own quirly, settled in a sitting position on the warm ground.

Zak looked at Tesoro, wondering how he had acquired his name. Tesoro meant "treasure" in Spanish. It was an odd sobriquet for a seasoned Apache warrior. Tesoro looked at him with cold ebony eyes.

"Raise your shirt, Tesoro," Anillo said.

Tesoro, his cigarette dangling from his lips, lifted his worn cotton shirt, almost proudly, Zak thought.

Zak stared at Tesoro's bare chest in disbelief.

The wounds were fresh. He had seen similar scars before, on warriors who had participated in the Sun Dance on the plains of the Dakotas, rips in their skin where they had impaled hooks that tore loose as they danced around a pole, connected to it with long leather thongs.

But these wounds were different. They were not scars made from hooks or knives. They were burns, and he had seen the likes of these before, as well. On his father's body after Ben Trask had tortured him by jabbing a red hot poker into his flesh.

The burn marks were the same, and some were scabbed over. Others were pocks with new flesh growing in the depressions. Tesoro had been tortured over a period of time. These burns were not made in a single day or night, but over a period of days, or perhaps even weeks.

"What do you see?" Anillo asked, plumes of smoke jetting from his nostrils and out the corners of his mouth.

"Burns," Zak said. "Iron burns."

Tesoro nodded and let his shirt fall back into place.

Somehow, Zak knew the burns were not connected to some Apache ritual or religious ceremony. Tesoro, he was sure, had been tortured.

"A man burned him with hot iron," Zak said. "A man who wanted Tesoro to tell him something."

"*Verdad*," Anillo said. "This is true."

"A white man burned Tesoro," Zak said. "Does Tesoro know the name of this man?"

"He knows the name of the man," Anillo said. "Do you know the name of this man?"

"Is the name difficult for the Apache to say?"

"Yes. It is hard to say this name," Anillo said.

"Trask," Zak said. "Ben Trask."

A light came into Tesoro's eyes when he heard the name. That was the only sign that he recognized it. His features remained stoic.

"Terask," Anillo said. "Ben, yes."

"A bad man," Zak said. "This is one I hunt. This is a man I would kill."

"How do you know this was the man who burned Tesoro with hot iron?"

"He did the same to my father," Zak said. "And then he killed my father."

"Ah. And why did Terask do this to your father?"

"Gold. My father had gold. Trask wanted it."

"That is why this man burned Tesoro," Anillo said.

"Does Tesoro have gold?" Zak asked.

Other Apaches had drifted down to listen. They made a ring around the three men on the ground. One still stood at the top, along with those guarding the ponies. He was standing watch, his head turning in all directions. Like an antelope guarding its herd, Zak thought.

Anillo and Tesoro exchanged glances.

"It is the name of Tesoro. Terask, he think maybe Tesoro has gold."

"Treasure," Zak said in English, more to himself than to either Anillo or Tesoro.

Anillo nodded. "Yes. Tesoro. Treasure. He captured Tesoro and he burned him with the iron to make him tell where Apache hides gold."

Zak knew such rumors had abounded for years, going all the way back to the Conquistadors from Spain who believed there were cities of gold in the New World. Ben Trask would most certainly be interested in such rumors, and probably believed them to be true. There was gold in Apache country. Whether any of the tribes had accumulated some of that gold was a question that had been debated and mulled over for many years.

"Tesoro did not tell him," Zak said.

"Tesoro does not know."

"Do the Apaches have gold?" Zak asked.

Anillo's face did not change expression.

"You ask a question many white men ask."

"But you do not answer," Zak said.

"Gold makes white men mad. It is just something that is in the earth, like rock or cactus, like trees or like water. The Apache does not seek gold. If he finds it, he hides it from the white man because he knows the yellow metal makes the white man crazy."

"Trask did not kill Tesoro. Why?"

"Tesoro was like the snake in the night. He moved so quiet. The white men did not see him. He ran away. He ran for many days. Now he, too, would kill Terask if he sees him."

"Tesoro," Zak said, addressing the silent Apache, "do you hunt Trask?"

Tesoro opened his mouth. He made a croaking sound in his throat.

Zak saw that his tongue had been cut out.

"When Tesoro would not tell Terask where the Apache hides the gold, he cut out the tongue of Tesoro," Anillo said. "The white men got drunk and they laughed. They played with the tongue of Tesoro while Tesoro swallowed his own blood and became the snake that hides in the grass and crawls away in the night."

"*Quanto lamento lo que ha pasado con Tesoro*," Zak said. I'm sorry for what happened to Tesoro.

"*No hay de que*," Anillo said. It is nothing. "Tesoro is strong. One day he will cut the throat of Terask. I will piss in his mouth before that."

"How do you know the name of Trask, if Tesoro cannot speak?"

"The Mexican you killed. He say the name. Terask was here. He bring horses, supplies, men. We watch. We hear. Trask chase us. He catch Tesoro."

"Do you know where Trask is?" Zak asked.

Anillo shook his head.

"The little adobe you burned. There are more of these *casitas*." He slowly swung his raised arm in a wide sweep to take in all of the country. "They are here and they are there. Terask he goes to them, but he does not stay long. I think he goes to Tucson."

"You will not go to Tucson," Zak said.

Anillo shook his head.

"That is a town of the white man. The Apache does not go there. The Chiricahua does not go there."

"I will go there. I will find Trask. If I take him alive, I will bring him to you. But I do not know where to find you."

"You bring Terask. We will find you, Cody."

Zak finished his smoke and stood up. Anillo and Tesoro stood up, too. The three men looked at each other, wordless in their understanding of each other.

"I go now," Zak said, and turned toward his horse.

"*Vaya con Dios*," Anillo said.

Zak pulled himself up into the saddle.

He repeated the phrase to Anillo and Tesoro.

As he rode away, he muttered to himself, "I didn't know the Apache believed in God."

And he smiled as he said it.

There was a lot he did not know about the Apache.

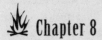 **Chapter 8**

Ben Trask poured two fingers of whiskey into Hiram Ferguson's glass.

"Maybe this will calm your nerves, Hiram," Trask said. "You're as jumpy as a long-tailed cat in a room full of rocking chairs."

Ferguson's hands shook as he lifted the glass to his lips. He was almost as big a man as Trask, but he was soft, flabby, with pudgy lips, jowls like a basset hound's, and at least three chins under a round moon face. Trask was all hard muscle, half a foot taller than Ferguson, with a lean, angular face, and a hooked nose that looked as if it had been carved out of hickory with a hatchet. Wind and sun had burnished his features to a rich brown tan. His pale blue eyes were almost gray, portraying no emotion, like the eyes of a dead fish.

"That's what you wanted, Hiram, wasn't it? Get the army to chase out the Chiricahua?"

"Yeah, but we wanted to make 'em mad that the Apaches were killin' civilians, burnin' down their homes, rapin' their women. I never called on you to go after soldiers. Shit almighty, Ben. You done took one giant step. In the wrong direction, to my way of thinkin'."

"Hiram, you got nowhere with them tactics. Now you got that damned Jeffords smokin' the peace pipe with Cochise and his whole gang. Then you go to the army mollycoddlin' every red nigger from the Rio Grande to Santa Fe."

"They're even talkin' about namin' a fort after them bastards," Ferguson said.

They were sitting in the Cantina Escobar, not far from Ferguson's Stage & Freight Company. Most of the men inside were as anti-Apache as Ferguson, including the six Mexicans who had dressed up like Chiricahua and killed the two soldiers.

The others were local ranchers and their hands. Most of these were standing at the long bar, quaffing beer and eating pickled sausages prepared by Antonio Escobar's wife, Lucinda, who also cooked *bistec, frijoles refritos, juevos, papas, puerco,* and anything else a hungry man might ask for. The smells from the kitchen were not overpowered by the scent of smoke and whiskey and mescal, tequila and fresh sawdust on the dirt floor hauled in from the nearby lumberyard and sawmill. The tables were small, except for one, which was used by card players and sat in the front corner to make room for all the tables. There was no music on most nights, but sometimes Lucinda's brother would bring his guitar and sing sad Mexican folksongs on holidays when the cantina was occupied largely by Mexican vaqueros. This was not one of those nights, and the crowd was equally divided between Mexicans and *norteamericanos.*

"Look, Hiram, you wanted me to bring the army

down on the Apaches. That's why I staged that
attack on one of your stages to make it look like
the Apaches were on the warpath. By now, that
gal has told every woman in that fort about that
savage Indian attack."

"Speakin' of that, where in hell is Jenkins?" Ferguson asked. "He should have been back from
Bowie this afternoon."

"Who knows?" Trask said. "I'm wondering how
you're doing with O'Hara. You still got him over
at the freight yard?"

"So far, he won't talk."

"He knows where every Apache camp is from
here to the San Simon. Maybe you ought to let
me work him over. And while we're at it, what's
the difference between you kidnapping a cavalry
officer and my bunch putting out the lamps on a
couple of soldier boys? I'd like a crack at O'Hara. I
could make him talk like a damned magpie."

"No," Ferguson said. "I've seen your work, Ben.
We'll get what we need out of him."

"When?"

"By tomorrow. His sis was on that stage Jenkins
took out of here to Fort Bowie. He sets store by
her. I'm going to tell him we'll grab her and put the
boots to her if he doesn't tell us what we want to
know."

"Just what are you doing to make O'Hara tell us
where those Apaches are holed up?"

"The lieutenant's bobbing for apples," Ferguson
said.

"Huh?"

"You wanta see? Finish up and we'll walk over
to the office."

"Damned right I want to see," Trask said.

He finished his whiskey, stood up.

Ferguson swallowed the last of his drink.

"See you later, boys," Trask said to the Mexicans still drinking at the tables, their heads and shoulders bathed in lamplight and blue smoke. He laid some bills on the table, picked up the bottle, held it against the light to see how much whiskey was left. He grunted in satisfaction.

The two men walked out of the cantina and toward the freight office. Its windows sprayed orange light on the porch. A man with a scattergun stood in the shadows beneath the eaves, while another, with a rifle, paced back and forth between the corrals and the office building, his boots crunching on sand and gravel. The shotgun man worked for Ferguson. His name was Lou Grissom. The man with the rifle was one of his own, Al Deets, as hard as they came, not a soft bone in him.

"Al," Trask said. "In the dark you got to shoot low."

"Yeah, Ben," Deets said. "Low and off to one side."

Trask laughed as they clumped up the steps onto the porch. Grissom just stood there, like a mute statue. He wasn't at all friendly, Trask thought, and that was the kind of man you needed to stand guard with a Greener chocked up with buckshot.

Ted O'Hara sat in a chair in a back room, stripped of his shirt, his arms and legs bound with manila rope. He looked haggard in the sallow light from a single lantern dangling from an overhead rafter. Two men stood on either side of him, bracing him against the chair back so he wouldn't fall forward.

In front of O'Hara sat a wooden tub filled with water. O'Hara's face and hair were wet, his eyes closed, his head drooping downward so that his chin almost rested on his chest.

"He asleep?" Ferguson said.

"Tryin'," one of the men, Jesse Bob Cavins, said.

"He say anything 'bout them Apache hideouts?" Ferguson asked the other man, a gaunt stringy hardcase named Willy Rawlins.

"Nope. He's just swallered a lot of water, Hiram." Rawlins had a West Texas drawl you could cut with a butcher knife if you laid it on a chunk of wood.

"Nothing?" Trask said, a scowl forming on his face.

"Nary," Rawlins said.

"Says he don't know nothin'," Cavins said, "and we near drowneded him ten minutes ago."

"He have any papers on him?" Trask asked. "Maps, stuff like that?"

"On that table over yonder," Cavins said, nodding in the direction of a table next to a rolltop desk against one wall.

Trask walked over to the table and picked up an army pouch. He opened it, spread the contents out on the tabletop. Ferguson strode up to stand beside him.

"None of that made any sense to us," Hiram said. "Army stuff."

"You ever in the army, Hiram?"

"Nope. Not as a regular. I hauled freight out of Santa Fe and Taos up to Pueblo and Denver. Warn't no war up yonder."

Trask opened a folded paper and laid it out flat.

"This here's a field map," he said. "If you know how to read 'em, you can find out where you are. Or, in this case, where our young Lieutenant O'Hara has been."

"Lot of gibberish to me," Ferguson said.

"There's numbers on it, in different places."

"Don't make no sense."

"No, not to you and me. But I'll bet O'Hara there knows what they mean. Did you show him the map? Ask him about it?"

Ferguson looked at the two men flanking O'Hara. They both shook their heads.

"Why not?" Trask asked.

"Yeah, why not?" Ferguson asked.

"We just asked him what you told us to ask him, Hiram."

"And what was that?" Trask wanted to know, a warning tic beginning to quiver along his jawline.

"Where in hell them Apaches' camps was," Rawlins said.

"We asked him about Cochise, too," Cavins said, a defensive tone to his voice.

"What did he say to those questions?" The tic in Trask's facial muscles subsided as his jaw hardened. In the silence, the men could almost hear Trask's teeth grind together.

"He said he didn't know," Rawlins said.

"He said he was on the scout, follerin' orders is all." Cavins was on the verge of becoming belligerent, and Ferguson shot him a warning glance.

Trask huffed in a breath as if he was building up steam inside him. But he remained calm. He knew men. These would be no trouble. Not Cavins nor Rawlins, not even Ferguson. Trask had observed

men like these all his life, and men like O'Hara,
as well. He knew the realms of darkness they all
harbored. He knew their fears. Torturing men had
given him insights that few other men ever even
thought about. But he also knew when torture
would fail, result only in silence or death.

O'Hara had been Ferguson's idea, but then he
had inside information, a conduit of some kind
that led straight into Fort Bowie. An inside man. A
man who hated Apaches as much as he did. Hiram
knew someone high up in the military, at the post,
who knew what O'Hara was scouting. But Hiram
didn't know how to dig that information out of
a man like O'Hara, a soldier who held to higher
standards than he did.

"Mind if I take a crack at soldier boy?" Trask
said. "You got any coffee you can make in here?"

"Long as you don't mark him up none, Trask,"
Ferguson said. "Willy, you put on some Arbuckle's.
Bob, get some kindlin' started in that potbelly."

Rawlins walked over to a sideboard built into
the wall. Nearby was a potbellied stove with a flat
round lid on top. Cavins knelt down and opened
the door, picked up a stick of kindling wood and
poked around in the ashes.

"Deader'n hell," he said. "Nary a coal." Then he
set about making a fire.

Rawlins rattled a pot against another, set out the
one that made coffee, lifted the lid. He opened an
airtight of Arbuckle's coffee, releasing the aroma of
cinnamon. He dipped grinds into the pot, replaced
the lid.

"What do you aim to do, Ben?" Ferguson asked.

"Perk this guy up some, first off."

Trask walked over to O'Hara, the map in his hands. He knelt down in front of the lieutenant, put his hand on O'Hara's chin, tilted his head back up. O'Hara's eyelids fluttered open. His blue eyes were watery, unfocused.

"You awake, Lieutenant O'Hara? We're not going to put your face in the water no more, son. We just want to talk."

O'Hara opened his eyes wider, stared at Trask.

"Not going to tell you anything."

"That's all right. You've been through hell, and it don't make no difference no more. We found your map. It tells us what we want to know."

"Map?"

Trask held up the map. O'Hara looked down at it.

"This field map we found on you. You recognize it?"

"No," O'Hara said.

"That's fine. It's got numbers on it. Know what they mean?"

"No."

Trask smiled. "Well, take a good look, Lieutenant. Maybe you do."

O'Hara turned his head away. He struggled with his bonds, then gave up fighting it. They didn't loosen.

"Sir, you'll pay for this," he said. "Holding me prisoner. The army will probably hang you."

"Oh, I don't think so. You're not hurt, are you? You maybe swallered some water, got your hair wet, is all."

"I was kidnapped. At gunpoint."

"Not by me."

"Who are you?" O'Hara asked.

"That's not important. I came to help you. You want to go back to Fort Bowie all in one piece. Your sis is there, waiting for you."

"Colleen?"

"Yeah, I guess that's her name."

O'Hara breathed a sigh, gulped in air. His eyes began to clear. "How do you know this?"

"Why, she rode this man's stage to Fort Bowie. There were two soldiers with her. Some damned Apaches attacked the stage. Killed and scalped the two soldiers, but the driver got her away and set her down safe in Fort Bowie. Ain't that right, Hiram?"

"Sure is."

"So, you can go back there, too. I just thought you might want to help me with this map here."

"No. I can't help you. Those numbers don't mean anything to me."

Trask stood up. O'Hara followed him with his gaze, looked up at him.

Trask's manner had changed. The smile was gone, the face hard again.

"Listen to me, you sonofabitch," Trask said, his voice a husky rasp, "if you don't want to see me cut your sister's throat, right here, right in front of you, you'd better tell me what these numbers on the map mean. Are they Apache camps?"

Before O'Hara could answer, there was a commotion outside. Hoofbeats and the rumble of a wagon or coach. A moment later Lou Grissom blasted through the door as if he were on fire.

"Mr. Ferguson, Jenkins's coach just rolled in."

"Jenkins all right?"

"I don't know. He ain't drivin' it."

"Well, who the hell is?" Ferguson snapped.

"Somebody wearing a United States Army uniform, and they's an army escort pullin' up right with him."

"Shit," Ferguson said.

O'Hara opened his mouth as if to yell. Trask clamped a hand over his mouth, drew his pistol, held it like a hammer and brought it down hard on top of O'Hara's head. There was a sharp crack and O'Hara's head dropped like a sash weight as he fell unconscious.

"Just don't let the bastards in here, Hiram," Trask said. "Get out there and find out what's going on."

Ferguson needed no urging. He was out the door a second or two later, Grissom on his heels.

Trask stared after them. Cavins and Rawlins stood frozen by the stove. The coffeepot burbled, spewed steam into the air.

Trask put a finger to his lips and holstered his pistol.

There was a silence in the room as if no one was there.

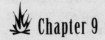 **Chapter 9**

The two men continued to argue. They had been at it ever since the wagon came through, changed horses, and left them way out in the middle of that bleak nowhere. A place that had no name. A way station between Tucson and Fort Bowie, but not on any known trail or road that either man knew of or gave a damn about. Someplace on the distant edge of a ranch, they figured, a line shack no longer used by any white man.

A dust devil swirled across the flat above the spring, and the horses in the pole corral neighed, flattened their ears at the sound, like a great whisper in a hollow room. Miles of nothingness stretched out in all directions around the homely adobe, and Larry Tolliver, yoked with two wooden pails of springwater, paused to watch the swirling dust as if that was an event to break the monotony, a rent in the fabric of sameness that dogged his days in isolation.

Danny Grubb sat outside the adobe shack, whittling on a piece of mesquite, his eyes squinted against the glare of the falling sun, a wad of plug tobacco bulging out his cheek like some hidden growth distorting his lean, angular face. The *whick whick* of the knife blade was the only sound in his mindless mind, the blond and gray curls of the shaven wood falling to the parched ground like locks on a barbershop floor.

Tolliver, puffing from exertion, slipped the yoke from his shoulders and set the pails down in front of Grubb. The water sloshed over the rims, stained the ground for a second before it disappeared, sucked up by the wind and sucked down by the thirsty earth, like ink vanishing under the pressure of a blotter.

"Go on ahead, Larry, spill ever' damn drop of that water," Grubb said.

"While you sit on your skinny ass, Danny."

"Hell, I might make a whistle outta this stick of mesquite and play you a tune come dark."

"You can stick that whistle square up your ass, Danny."

"I might stick it up yours, you keep flappin' your sorry mouth."

"You could carry this water inside, out of the dust."

"I could, but I been cuttin' the wood. It'll be colder'n a well-digger's ass once that sun goes down."

The incoming wagon had brought them two cords of firewood. Danny had been splitting sticks of kindling for their cookstove, so he didn't see where Tolliver had any room for complaints. He had also fed the six horses in the corral. The wagon had also brought grain. When it returned, with

Rawlins and Cavins, it carried their prisoner, one
Ted O'Hara, an army lieutenant wearing shabby
civilian clothes. Grissom had been with them, too,
and Danny had begged him to stay at the shack
and let him go back with the wagon into Tucson.

"I got my orders, Danny," Grissom had said.
"Hiram says you boys got to stay another month."

"What for?"

"For thirty a month and found," Grissom had
said with a vicious little laugh that still irritated
Danny when he thought about it. Everything irritated him, especially Tolliver.

"Who's going to fix supper?" Danny asked.

"My turn, I reckon," Tolliver said.

"My belly hurts already."

"Look, Danny, I don't like bein' out here
anymore'n you do, but we got to make the best of
it. You don't like it, you can slap a saddle on one of
them horses and ride on back to town."

"When I think of Rawlins and Cavins swillin'
down beer and whiskey in the cantina," Danny
said, "I get plumb burned. They ought to try this
shit for a time."

"Hiram said we'd take turns. They might come
back in a couple of weeks."

"That'll be the day," Danny said, and threw
down the stick of whittled wood, closed his Barlow
knife and stuck it in his pocket.

Larry Tolliver cooked supper and opened a can
of peaches. After they ate and Danny washed the
tin plates, the knives, forks, and spoons, they sat
outside. Larry smoked and Danny chewed on a cut
plug of tobacco. The sunset was as sweet as the

night was depressing. The bright clouds had turned
to ash and then faded to black as the sky sparkled
with stars and the wind turned chill.

"You hear anything?" Danny asked after a while.
He spat a plume of tobacco into the dust.

Larry watched the smoke from his cigarette twist
into ghostly shapes that resembled small animals
in the lantern light, snakes and mice and tiny gray
birds. They unfolded in the breezeless air like paint-
ings on parchment.

"Nope," he said. But he listened. It got spooky
out there at night, and they hadn't heard the coyotes sing as they usually did. There was a quiet that
made the silence seem loud.

There wasn't so much as the crunch of a boot
on sand, nor the clink of an overturned rock, but
there he was, standing in front of them, dressed all
in black like an undertaker, his eyes shaded by his
hat brim so that they couldn't see them. He wore a
big Walker Colt on his hip, and the way he stood
there, as if he had come out of nowhere, made both
men freeze as though thunderstruck.

"Just set there easy," Zak said, and his voice
carried authority. It was low-pitched and firm, vi-
brated in his throat with a hypnotizing hum. The
voice didn't even seem to come from him, but from
somewhere else, from somewhere above him.

Tolliver's throat went dry as the dirt under his
feet, but he managed to squeak out a question.

"Damn, where'd you come from?"

Zak said nothing. He looked at the two men.
Both were armed, but they didn't look ready to
defend anything they might have inside the adobe
or on their persons.

"Mister, you oughtn't walk up on a man like that," Grubb said. "You could get yourself killed for no good reason."

"I've been watching you two fellows," Zak said. "Had my eye on you since late afternoon. If ever I saw a couple of dunces, you two were they. I doubt if either of you could hit the broadside of a barn at five paces. But if words were bullets, you two would be champion shots. I haven't heard such arguing since I stayed with a married man and his wife up on the Judith."

"You been listenin' to us?" Tolliver said, gape-mouthed.

"Voices carry out here," Zak said. "A long way."

"Well, what you sneakin' around for?" Grubb said. "Spyin' on people like that. Ask me, you're the one ain't got good sense."

"I'll tell you why I stopped by, mister." Zak looked at Grubb. "Danny."

Danny recoiled in shock that the stranger knew his name. "Yeah? How come?" he said.

"There was a wagon come through here with a kidnapped soldier in it. I want you boys to tell me where it's going to wind up. I'll give you five seconds, Danny, and I'm counting real fast."

"Ain't none of your business," Tolliver said.

"Three," Zak said.

"What you gonna do if we don't tell you?" Danny asked.

"One of you I'm going to blow straight to hell," Zak said.

"Which one?" Danny asked.

"One second left."

"Jesus," Tolliver said, and he wasn't praying.

Danny, rattled, spoke first.

"Ferguson," he said.

Tolliver chimed in on the heels of Danny's one word statement.

"Edge of Tucson. You find Cantina Escobar, you'll see the freight company a stone's throw away."

"Either of you know a man named Ben Trask?"

The two men looked at each other, their expressions showing their bewilderment.

"Naw," they said, like a chorus of jackdaws.

"You know the soldier's name? The one that was in the wagon?"

"They called him O'Hara," Danny said. "Young feller. Still wet behind the ears."

"Tied up," Tolliver said.

"Where's the next station?"

"Huh?" Danny said.

"Is there another one of these 'dobes where that wagon was headed?"

"Two more," Tolliver said.

"You boys are out of business," Zak said. "As of right now. I'll leave you two horses. The rest I'm running off."

"You can't do that," Tolliver said. "They hang horse thieves in this country."

"I'm not stealing them. I'm just turning them loose. You got any apples inside that 'dobe?"

"Apples?" Danny said.

"Yeah, my horse likes apples."

Both men shook their heads.

"Does this look like a damned orchard?" Tolliver said, suddenly belligerent.

"I don't see no horse," Danny said.

Zak turned his head, gave a low whistle. Then he called, "Nox."

The black horse, his coat shining like dark water, came around the corner of the adobe, reins trailing. He ambled up to Zak, who rubbed the hollows over the horse's eyes, worried his topknot with massaging knuckles.

"I ought to burn you out," Zak said. "But I'm just going to turn those horses out and ride on."

He grabbed his reins, separated them, and draped the ends over the horse's neck, just in front of the saddle.

"Mister, you ain't running none of our horses off," Tolliver said. "I'm callin' you out."

Zak turned toward Tolliver and stared him straight in the eyes. He let his right hand slide easily down his horse's neck until it was parallel to the butt of his pistol.

Tolliver sat there, blinking. Under the brim of his grease-stained hat, his eyes glittered with lantern light and shadow. He screwed up his lips as if chewing on something distasteful. Seconds ticked by as the silence deepened into a great ocean tossing with soundless seas. Grubb swallowed and his Adam's apple bobbed, a sharp pointed spearhead beneath the skin.

"If you do," Zak finally said, "it'll be the last thing you call out."

"You don't scare me none," Tolliver said.

"You're going to hear two things, Tolliver," Zak said.

"Yeah?"

"One is the sound of my Walker Colt calling out your name. The other is old Angel Gabe blowing his trumpet, calling you to Judgment Day."

Tolliver snarled, uttered an oath under his breath. He came up into a crouch, his hand diving for his pistol. Danny sat there, trying to hold back his bowels, his face drained of color, leaving only the white stain of fear sprawling on his features.

Zak didn't take his eyes off Tolliver as his fingers grasped the butt of his pistol. Tolliver was pulling his own pistol from its holster. In that wink of eternity, it seemed as if it took hours for the barrel of the pistol to clear the sheath. In that split second, Tolliver's face mirrored his final thought: He was going to make it.

Zak's pistol seemed to leap into his hand, and when he thumbed back the hammer, the click made Danny jump inside his skin. Tolliver's barrel came clear and his thumb pressed down on the hammer to cock the single action.

Zak's Colt bellowed, spewing a bright orange flame, unburnt powder, and a .44 caliber lead projectile from its muzzle. The roar of the explosion was like a single thunderclap drowning out the sizzle of the bullet as it sped faster than the speed of sound, making a crack like a bullwhip just before it smashed into the center of Tolliver's chest with all the impact of a pile driver.

Tolliver's finger closed around the trigger, then went slack as he was slammed back against the wall of the adobe, a jet of blood spurting from his chest, a crimson fountain that drenched his belly and the crotch of his trousers. Danny put his arms up over his head and ducked as if to ward off the next shot that he was sure would come.

Tolliver slumped against the adobe. His pistol

slipped from his hand and made a dull thud as it struck the dirt. He stared a thousand yards without seeing anything but a blur, an afterglow of orange light burning into his brain.

Danny swallowed his tobacco. It made him sick and he pitched forward, vomiting it back up, along with the moil of his supper and whatever else was inside his tortured stomach.

Zak walked over, picked up Tolliver's pistol, stuck it inside his belt. He then lifted Grubb's pistol from its holster as Danny went through the throes of the dry heaves.

"I'm leaving you two horses. One for yourself, one to pack out that dead man there. You tell Ferguson and Trask I'm coming for them. And I'll ask you one more time, Danny, how many more of these line shacks between here and Tucson? The ones Ferguson is using."

A watery-eyed Danny looked up at Zak, wiped vomit from his chin.

"Two more, that I know of. Hell, I don't even know who you are," he croaked.

"The name's Cody."

Zak walked inside the adobe and kicked over the stove, threw the lantern onto the coals. Then he walked out, past Danny, and climbed into the saddle. He rode down to the corral, tied Nox to a pole, went inside. He ran all but two of the horses out and closed the gate. He looked up toward the flaming adobe and saw Danny pulling Tolliver's body away from the conflagration.

Zak untied the reins, pulled himself back up into the saddle.

He rode off through a shimmering band of firelight, into the night, following the wagon tracks. He heard the horses galloping away and the neighs of those left behind.

In the distance, across the vastness of night, the coyotes loosed their ribbons of song. And the moon rose over the horizon, bright and full, its shining face lighting his way long after he left the burning adobe behind.

And he felt as if his father were riding alongside him, speaking to him in the Ogallala tongue, the language of his mother.

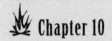 **Chapter 10**

General Grant sipped his whiskey, then signed the paper on his desk. He handed it to General Crook, who was seated on the other side, in a high-backed, upholstered chair that he was sure had come out of a medieval torture chamber. His sword jabbed him in the thigh, and the armrests were too small, too low.

"I want just you and me to know about this, George," Grant said.

"Understood, General."

Crook read the paper.

"You sign it, too," Grant said.

"Of course. Gladly.

Crook leaned over Grant's desk and lay the paper flat. Grant handed him a quill pen. George signed his name with a celeritous flourish.

"I don't want this man wearing a uniform," Grant said. "He might as well wear a red flag draped around him. No, Cody will be more useful to us if our enemies don't see a soldier walking up to them carrying a rifle and a sidearm. Give him rank, but disguise him as a civilian."

"As you wish, General," Crook said. "I'll make Zak Cody a colonel, fair enough?"

"Fair and appropriate, General Crook."

"This is the last thing I wanted to accomplish before I took the oath of the presidency," Grant said. *"I think Cody will prove himself out, don't you?"*

"I have no doubt, General."

That was the story Zak heard as told to him by General Crook when the general pinned the oak leaf clusters on his uniform.

"This is the last time you'll see these on your shoulders, Zak," Crook said. "Tomorrow, you'll be a civilian. I want you to see that the Indians of this country get a fair shake."

And that was how it had started. Those same thoughts recurred time and again in Cody's mind whenever he doubted himself or his mission.

Now, as he rode through the night, he wore the mantle Crook had placed on him and it was beginning to weigh heavy on him and give him an itch. He reported to no one, but he also had no guidance but his own. He hoped he was doing the right thing, but he was a tightrope walker working high above the crowd without a net.

Sometime before midnight he made a dry camp, no fire, grass for Nox, a small hill in the open, and hid his bedroll just below it. He ate for the first time that day, filling the hollow in his stomach with beef jerky, hardtack, and water. He was used to such fare, and going for long periods without food was no hardship. He had lived worse, in deep winter snows, high above the world in the Rocky Mountains or in the Paha Sapa, the sacred Black Hills.

If his father's spirit had ridden with him that night, it was the spirit of his mother that he felt now, as he lay under a canopy of stars with the light zephyrs whispering through the cholla and the yucca. He remembered looking up through the smoke hole of the tipi at night and seeing those same stars and how, over time, they journeyed in circles, the sacred circles so revered by the Lakota.

Her name was White Rain, and she told him once how she had come to be called by that appellation. She did not speak English well, but his father had taught her a few words because he loved her dearly and his Ogallala was not the best. Zak came to know both languages, and others, for his ear was tuned early to languages and dialects.

"When I was born," his mother told him, "my skin was so pale that the old woman who drew me from the belly of my mother said that I must have been washed by a white rain as I made the journey to this world."

"Your mother, was she Hunkpapa or Ogallala?"

"No, she had skin like mine. The red clay had been washed away. She was a captive girl, taken from the white eyes, and my father, War Shield, took her as his wife, as your father took me. My mother's Lakota name was Yellow Bead by the time she had grown into woman."

His father would not tell him much about his mother, and his few memories were hazy. He had only been with her until the Black Robe came and told his father he was going to take Zak away before he turned pure Indian. Black Robe told Russell Cody that there was a white woman at Bent's Fort who could raise the boy and teach him to read and write, to converse properly in the English language. Russell had reluctantly agreed after White

Rain died, when Zak was almost eleven years old.

He had never seen a man grieve so, as his father had, after his mother died. Russell worked the traplines long after the last rendezvous. The market for beaver had vanished, and most of the mountain men, the free trappers he lived and hunted with, had gone back to St. Louis or St. Joe, or died of sadness and old age.

"Pa," Zak had said, "why do you sit and stare at nothing for hours? And you cry at night. I hear you. I hear you call out her name."

"When White Rain left me, son, it felt like she took part of me with her. A big part. And I don't know how to get it back. When I look out at the world, there's a big empty spot where your ma once stood. Just an empty place wherever she walked."

"But I miss her, too, Pa."

"I know you do, Zak. You came out of her. You were a part of her. But she and me, we were just one person like. I don't know how to explain it no better'n that. She's done gone and I'm half a man."

"No, you ain't, Pa. You're the same."

"Outside, maybe. Not inside. She squeezed my heart, that woman. Squeezed it real hard whenever she smiled, whenever she put her hand on my arm, whenever she kissed me or lay by my side on the robe."

"You don't take me hunting no more, Pa, and I've had all that book learning. You sent me off with Black Robe and I wanted to be with you and Ma. I cried every night down at the fort. For a long time."

Russell put his arm on Zak's shoulder.

"I'm sorry son. I thought it was for the best."

"Maybe Ma don't want you to cry for her no more, Pa. Maybe she wants you to hunt with me, fish with me, 'stead of sittin' around this Sioux camp like one of the old ones with no teeth, just waiting to die."

"You got your ma's sensibility, son, I reckon. No, she wouldn't want me to be a lie-about-camp. She'd tell me to get up off my ass and make meat. But the trappin's all played out and the buffalo are as thin as the mist on the Rosebud. Ain't no life for me no more."

"Maybe I should just give up, too, then, Pa."

"Give up? I never said you should give up."

"Well, Ma's just as dead to me as she is to you. And now you might as well be dead, too. I come back and the braves are still talking about fighting the Crow and going after buffalo and making the Sun Dance. They're living in the past same as you. I learned that much when I was staying with Mrs. McKinney down at Bent's."

"I ain't give up." Stubborn old bastard. Beard stubble on his face like mold growing on rancid deer meat. Grease worried into his buckskins so deep it would never wash out, his moccasins full of sewed up holes, and half his beadwork, White Rain's beadwork, gone, the rest hanging on sinew thread, ready to fall into the dirt. His hair long and full of lice, dirty as a dog's hind leg.

"It looks like you have given up, Pa. I can't say it no plainer than that. You got old real fast, and next your teeth are going to fall out and you'll go blind staring at those empty places all the time. You got to get up off the robes and walk up the mountain with me, make the elk come to your call, the deer to your grunt. You got to hear the crack of your rifle again and see if the beaver have come back up on Lost Creek or over in the Bitterroots."

"I probably should give up."

"Pa, what's a 'squaw man'?"

"Where'd you hear that?"

"At the fort."

"That what they call me?"

Zak dipped his head and nodded.

"Well, that's from folks who just don't understand about livin' in the wilderness, son. They can call me a 'squaw man' all they like, but your ma was a special woman. And her ma, too. A white gal gets captured by an Injun and white folks don't want nothin' to do with 'em. Treat 'em like dirt. Worse than dirt, like cur dogs."

"Did you feel sorry for Ma?"

"No. I saw who she was. Where she come from. Her ma was just a child when she was took. She didn't know nothin' of white ways after a time. So she became a Sioux woman. It takes a mite of courage to change like that, give up what you was and become somethin' else."

"I think I know what you mean, Pa. I remember Curly Jack told me once that he became a mountain man because it was a better life than he had back in Tennessee. Said a man had to become an Indian if he was going to live through a winter in the mountains."

"Curly Jack said it right, Zak. We all came up here to trade with the red man. Once we tasted their life some, we got to lookin' at things different. We saw white people for what they was, and red people for what they was. We never learned any of that in no school down on the flat."

Zak thought about his schooling and realized that, while he had learned a lot about numbers and words and foreign countries, he had also learned that the white race hated the red men and didn't think of them as being human at all. He began to realize that he and his father lived in two different worlds. It was a sobering thought and went deep with him and stayed there all this time. That was probably why he and Crook had gotten along so well. Crook was a man who could look into both worlds and see the worth in each, as well as the worst in each.

He fell asleep thinking of White Rain and how his father had begun to recover and get back to life after that talk they had. They hunted and fished together, traveled the Rockies as carefree as a couple of kids let out from school for the summer, and they had grown close. That's when he found out that his father had been collecting gold in the Paha Sapa and saving it up, not for himself, but so that he could have a life of ease someday if he chose to live in the white world.

Neither of them had realized the path Zak would take, or that the country would take, going to war over slavery and states' rights, brother killing brother, father killing son, son killing father. Neither of them could foresee the future, but both knew what they both had lost when the beaver played out and White Rain died.

Zak could look back and see that all the signs were there, like signposts on roads that wound through the Badlands. Changes. New paths. The old ones blown over by wind and weather, the new ones dangerous, treacherous, dark.

Neither had seen a man like Ben Trask come down the trail, driven by greed, bent on torture and murder. Trask had intruded on their world as surely as the white man had intruded on the world of the Plains Indians and all the tribes in the nation. Such thoughts tightened things inside Zak, turned him hard inside, like the granite peaks of the Tetons, like a fist made out of stone.

The war changed him, too.

He had seen men torn to pieces by grapeshot and shrapnel, heard their screams and cries, seen the surgeons saw off gangrenous limbs and battlefields strewn with the bodies of young men, some with peach fuzz still on their faces, taken from life long before their allotted time, and it was all horror to see young men march into clouds of smoke and die by the hundreds.

Yet he had escaped harm, somehow, with bullets and minié balls whistling past his ear, bombs bursting all around him, horses shot from under him, and stronger men falling, left crippled for life. He thought of his mother and father often during those years, appreciating them both more than he ever had, missing them in those dark hours when he heard only the moans of the dead and dying while crickets struck up their orchestras in the blood-soaked grasses of woodland havens.

Zak fell asleep thinking back through those years, and feeling just as alone now as he had when the rattle of muskets and the clank of caissons were like a horde of metal insects marching across the land, leaving destruction in their wake, those desolate and deserted burnt lands where corpses stiffened in the sun and wild animals fed on them at night.

And the first kill strong in his mind, that bleak moment when he had shot a gray-clad soldier in the eye, seen him fall and later gaze up at him with that one sightless eye, his stomach churning with a nameless grief for the life he had taken, and the hollow feeling afterward, knowing something had changed inside him, something that could not be spelled out or described or explained.

His dreams picked up strands of these thoughts and wove them into a mysterious tapestry hanging in a great empty hall where the coyotes sang songs of the dead and White Rain smiled at him, great tears in her eyes, and his father stood knee-deep in a beaver pond filled with blood, holding up a rusted trap from which dangled a water snake with a human head that bore a strong resemblance to Ben Trask.

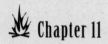 Chapter 11

Sergeant Leon Curtis bellowed down from the driver's seat.

"Who's in charge here?"

Hiram stepped off the porch. Trask stood there, eyeing the three soldiers he saw in the lantern light. Two on the seat, one on horseback. Two horses were on lead ropes behind the coach, unsaddled.

"I'm Hiram Ferguson. That's one of my coaches you've got there."

"Sergeant Curtis, sir. Returning your coach from Fort Bowie."

Curtis set the brake, wrapped the reins around the handle, picked up his carbine and started to climb down.

"Where in hell's my driver, Danny Jenkins?"

Curtis said nothing until his boots touched the ground.

"Inside the coach," Curtis said. A trooper untied his horse from the back of the coach, led it out, toward the sergeant.

"Jenkins," Ferguson called. "Danny? Come on out."

"He can't hear you no more," Curtis said.

"Huh?"

"The man in that coach is dead. Been embalmed and everything by the post surgeon."

"Dead? How? Somebody kill him?"

"Yes sir, somebody sure killed him."

"Who?" Ferguson asked.

"Man drove the coach into the fort with the lady come to teach the Injun women and children. He shot Jenkins. Said it was self-defense."

"Damn it, Sergeant, I demand to know who killed my driver."

"Man name of Cody. Zak Cody."

Ferguson shook his head. "Who in hell is this Cody? I never heard of him."

"Well, sir, we sure as hell heard of him. The man has quite a reputation. None of it proved, of course. But I wouldn't want to go up against him. Your man Jenkins had the drop on him, according to the ladies who heard the story from Miss O'Hara, and this Cody feller shot him plumb dead."

"Shit," Ferguson said. He did not look up on the porch where Trask stood. But he could feel Trask's eyes on his back, burning holes in it.

Curtis pulled a sheet of paper from his pocket, handed it to Ferguson.

"What's this?" Ferguson asked.

"A receipt, sir," Curtis answered. "For the coach. To show that I delivered it."

Ferguson held the paper up to the light as Curtis produced a pencil, held it out for him. Ferguson signed the paper and handed it back to the sergeant.

"That all?" Ferguson asked, anxious to open the coach.

"No, sir." Curtis pulled an envelope from inside his tunic, handed it to Ferguson. "From the acting commandant."

The packet was sealed with wax, oilcloth folded over. It rattled when Ferguson took it.

Curtis took the reins of his horse, mounted it stiff-necked, his back perfectly straight. He did not salute as he turned his horse, joined the other two soldiers. They rode off toward the town, vanished into the night. When the hoofbeats of their horses faded into the silence of night, Ferguson walked over to the coach and opened the door.

"Damn," he said, peering through the gloom.

It looked like a package, a bundle. Something wrapped in burlap and bound with twine. He knew what it was. He could smell the decomposing body even through the formaldehyde and the crushed mint leaves in a sack tied around the feet, dangling down from the seat.

"What is it?" Trask asked, not moving from the porch.

"It's Jenkins. Dead. Embalmed, I guess."

"Shit," Trask said as Ferguson turned away, then nodded to Grissom. "Put him somewhere, Lou. We'll bury him in the morning."

Ferguson walked back to the porch, climbed the steps. He held the oilcloth packet in his hands, unopened.

"What you got there, Hiram?" Trask asked.

"I don't know. Something from Fort Bowie, I reckon."

"Let's go inside," Trask said. "Find out what it is."

They entered the office. O'Hara sat there, staring at them.

"You want me to give him some of that coffee, Hiram?" Cavins said. "It's ready."

Ferguson looked at Trask, who nodded. Cavins turned and walked to the stove, lifted the pot and poured steaming coffee into a tin cup. He carried it back to O'Hara as Ferguson broke the seal on the packet, opened it.

He read it while O'Hara blew on the coffee to cool it as Cavins held the cup up to his mouth.

Ferguson read the letter. It was not written on official U.S. Army stationery and it was unsigned. But he knew who had written it.

"What's it say?" Trask said, eyeing Ferguson.

"Do you know a man named Cody? The one the sergeant said killed Jenkins."

Trask stiffened. His jaw hardened and a glint sparked in his narrowed eyes.

"I know him."

"He killed Danny Jenkins, all right, says here, just like the sergeant said. And Cody drove O'Hara's sis to the fort."

O'Hara's eyes widened. Trask glanced at him, then took Ferguson by the arm.

"Outside," he growled. "We got to talk."

O'Hara's face softened as he watched the two men go back outside and stand on the porch, out of earshot. He could hear only a murmur of voices, see their shadowed forms in silhouette.

"What else does it say, Hiram?"

"Read it yourself."

"Who's it from?" Trask asked as Ferguson handed him the letter.

"That's for me to know right now. Someone at the fort."

"Fine." Trask read the letter, let out a deep sigh.

"Gives you something to use on O'Hara in there," Ferguson said, licking his lips. There was still a faint taste of whiskey on them.

"Yeah. I think we'll find out what we want to know about that map we found on O'Hara." Trask paused, then handed the letter back to Ferguson. "Want to ask you something, though."

"Go ahead."

"How come you don't want me to burn the information out of O'Hara? You know we're going to have to kill him."

"I know," Ferguson said. "But it's got to look like Injuns, Apaches, done him in. If he's got burn marks on him from a hot poker, the army won't buy it. He's got to look like he was kilt by Apaches."

"My way is quicker. Surer."

"We have to play the hand my way, Ben. Trust me."

"All right. Let's see if O'Hara will tell us what we want to know."

"You going to use his sister?"

"That's what the letter says."

Ferguson nodded. He had read the words. "You can tell your prisoner that if he doesn't divulge what he knows about the enemy, that his sister will forfeit her life after being tortured by savage Indians." Carefully worded. No names. Formal, stiff. But that was the man's way, the one who had written the letter. And Ferguson knew that he meant what he said.

"Let's see what O'Hara has to say about that map," Ferguson said. "You put it to him about his sister."

Trask smiled.

The two men walked inside. Ferguson put the letter back in its packet, folded it and stuck it in a back pocket of his trousers.

"Untie O'Hara," Trask said to Cavins.

"You sure?" Cavins held the cup of coffee suspended above the prisoner.

"Yeah. He's not going anywhere and I want to talk to the lieutenant. He's going to need his hands to show me things on that map."

"I reckon," Cavins said, "if it's all right with Mr. Ferguson."

"Go ahead," Hiram said.

Trask took the cup from Cavins, watched as he untied O'Hara.

"Can you stand up?" Trask asked. He shoved the tub of water out of the way with his foot.

O'Hara, freed from his bindings, flexed his hands and arms, moved his legs. He stood up on wobbly legs.

"Good," Trask said. "Feel like talking with me now? You don't have much choice."

"I can't divulge any information pertaining to my military duties."

"Oh, I think you can, Lieutenant. If your sister's life is at stake. What's her name? Colleen? Yes, Colleen. We can see to it that some terrible things happen to her if you don't play our cards."

O'Hara's face drained of color. "You—You have my sister?"

Trask and Ferguson exchanged glances.

"Yeah, we do," Ferguson said.

Trask smiled at the smooth deception.

"All I want you to do, O'Hara," he said, "is tell

me what those numbers mean on that map. Did you draw it?"

"No, I'm not a cartographer."

"But you wrote the numbers on it?"

"I might have."

"Let's take a look," Trask said, grabbing O'Hara by the arm and leading him over to the table. He spread the map out, pointed to a spot marked with an X, west of the San Simon River.

O'Hara stared down at the map with its X's and numerals.

"That spot there, for instance," Trask said. "You write down them numbers?"

O'Hara drew in a breath, moved his head as if to clear it.

"Yes, I wrote the numbers there."

"Is that an Apache camp? One of their hidden strongholds?"

"Yes, it is," O'Hara said tightly, as if the words were being forced out of his mouth.

"What's this twenty-five mean? Right under the X, and the number under that, ten?"

O'Hara didn't answer right away.

"Means twenty-five braves. Number under it designates women and children."

"Can you find this place?' Trask said.

"Maybe."

"Well, you're damned sure going to, O'Hara," Trask said.

He turned to Ferguson.

"It's all laid out here, Hiram. All the Apache camps. We could sneak up on 'em and do what the army won't do, kill every damned one of 'em."

"I don't know if we have enough men, Ben."

"Won't take many. We pick up the men you got at those relay stations and swoop down on the camps and clean out every nest of rattlesnakes on this here map."

"Tall order."

"We have the advantage," Trask said.

"How's that?" Ferguson said.

"The Apaches won't know we're coming."

"What if we run into soldiers?"

"We tell 'em we're a hunting party. They can't cover all that ground, and they don't have the map. We do. And O'Hara here is going to lead us right to them."

"What if they recognize him?" Ferguson asked.

"I can take care of that, Hiram. His own mother wouldn't recognize him when I get through with him."

"What do you mean to do, Ben?"

Trask smiled. "Dress him up like one of my Mexicans, put a sombrero and a serape on him, sandals, dye his hair coal black."

"It might work."

Trask looked at O'Hara. He touched a finger to his blond hair.

"You're going to make one hell of a Mexican, Pedro," Trask said.

Then he laughed as O'Hara's eyes sparked with anger.

O'Hara shot out an arm, reached for the map on the table.

Trask drove a fist straight into O'Hara's temple, knocking him to the floor.

"Don't get up too quick, O'Hara," Trask said. "Or I'll give you an even bigger wallop." To Cavins he said, "Tie the bastard back up until morning. That's when we'll do the decorating and turn this soldier into a peon."

Ferguson shrank away from Trask, sucked in a breath.

He had seen violence before, but Trask really liked it. The man was like a coiled spring, ready to lash out at anyone who stood in his way. Yes, he wanted the Apaches cleared out of the country, but he began to wonder if he hadn't made a mistake in bringing Trask out from Santa Fe. The man had a thirst for blood that was insatiable.

Trask fixed Ferguson with a look.

"Don't worry, Hiram. The end always justifies the means."

And there was that smile again on Trask's face.

It sent shivers up and down Ferguson's spine.

🌵 Chapter 12

The land shimmered under the furnace blaze of the sun. Lakes danced and disappeared, water images rose and fell like falls, evaporated as Zak approached them, emerged farther on, shrank away in shining rivulets, trickled through the rocks and cactus and flowed along flats, puddled among the hillocks and vanished like fairy lights on a desolate moor. He was sweating and Nox's black coat shone like polished ebony while his tail flicked at flies.

Zak saw the station from afar and it, too, appeared and disappeared like some mirage as the land dipped and rose like some frozen ocean of sand and rock. Wagon tracks streamed toward the dwelling for some distance, but vanished among the low rocky hills that stood between him and the dwelling. Rather than follow the tracks through the hills, he chose to climb each one to afford himself a better view of the land ahead.

And the land he had left behind.

For Zak had the distinct feeling that he was being followed. He had looked over his shoulder more than once, but saw no sign of anyone on his trail. Yet the feeling persisted, and he knew, from long

experience, that such feelings were valid. A man
stayed alive because he paid attention to his in-
stincts, those gut feelings that something was not
quite right. In a room full of people, you could
stare at the back of a man's head for only so long.
Sooner or later that man would turn around and
return the stare. He had seen this too often to
ignore it.

For the past few miles he had felt someone staring at the back of his head. Not literally, of course,
but he had a strong hunch that even out there in all
that emptiness, he was not alone.

Nox climbed the first hill, paralleling the wagon
tracks. Zak fought off the compulsion to turn
around when he reached the top. Instead he started
down the other side until he was well past the
summit. Then he turned Nox and rode back up,
spurring the horse to scramble up the slope with
some speed. At the top, he scanned his backtrail,
his keen eyes searching every square inch of terrain
for any sign of movement.

A hawk sailed low over the ground, dragging
its rumpled shadow along as it searched for prey.
A pair of gray doves cut across the hawk's course
with whistling wings. A yucca swayed gently in the
breeze. A lizard sunned itself on a nearby rock, its
eyes blinking, its tail switching. He saw no other
movement, but something caught his eye and he
stared at it for a long time.

Shapes in the desert could fool a man. A shadow
next to a yucca could resemble a man sitting next
to it, or sprawled alongside. Rocks could become
human heads, poking up from shallow depressions

in the earth. A dark clump of rocks could appear as a horse standing still.

Zak looked for these illusions and discounted most of them in the space of a few seconds.

But just beyond a yucca and some brush, ocotillo and prickly pear, there was something, and he stared at it for a long time. It looked like the very top of a horse's head, two ears and a topknot. It did not move, but still it held his steady, piercing gaze.

Could a horse hold still for that long? Zak began counting the seconds. He counted to thirty, and still the odd shape did not move. He looked away for a moment, then slowly turned his head back once more to that same spot.

Whatever had been there was now gone.

Was he imagining things? Did he really see that shape, or was it just another illusion of light and shadow?

The image did not reappear, although Zak stared in that direction for several more seconds. Finally, he turned Nox and rode back over the hillock and down onto the flat. There was a jumble of hills all around him and he threaded his way through them before topping another. At the summit, though, he had less of a view than he'd had on the first hill and he did not linger. As he rode down the other side, movement caught his eye and he reined up, stabbed his hand toward the butt of his pistol.

"Do not shoot. I mean you no harm." The voice was oddly accented, low and timbrous.

Zak let his hand hover just above the butt of the Walker Colt.

"Show yourself," he said. He realized that he had seen the shadow of something off to his right, nothing of substance. He saw it again, the top of a yucca, torn off, sticking straight out from behind the hill. As he watched, it shook gently, then fell to the ground. A moment later a horse, a small horse, no more than fourteen hands high, emerged from behind the hillock. It was saddled and shod and carried a small, dark-skinned man dressed in old duck pants, a linsey-woolsey shirt, a blue bandanna around his neck. He wore a sidearm, and the butt of a rifle jutted from a scabbard attached to his worn Santa Fe saddle.

"You have been following me," Zak said.

"Yes, I have been following you, because I see what you are doing. What you have done."

"Who are you?" Zak asked.

"I am called Chama. Jimmy Chama."

"You are not a Mexican."

"No. I am Apache."

"Full blood?"

The man rode up close, shook his head. He wore a crumpled felt hat that had seen better days. But it kept the sun out of his eyes, which were dark brown. His hair was coal black, cut short on the sides, streamed down his neck in straight spikes in the back.

"My father was a Mexican," he said. "My mother was a Mescalero."

"You're in Chiricahua country, Jimmy."

Jimmy smiled. "I know. I have friends here. Not many, but a few."

"What brings you on my track?"

"I am on the same track. I am an army scout and

interpreter. I was sent with Lieutenant O'Hara to look for Chiricahua camps along the San Simon."

"Were you with him when he was kidnapped?"

"No. I was on a scout. When I returned, he was gone. I was sent to track those who took him."

"And the army?"

"They come. I leave sign for them. But as long as it does not rain, they can follow the wagon tracks, too."

"How many troops?"

"A dozen. But a courier was sent to Fort Bowie. There will be more."

"Are you sure?" Zak asked.

Chama cocked his head and a quizzical look spread over his face. "Why do you ask this?"

Zak shrugged. "I don't know. I have the feeling that things are not quite right at Fort Bowie."

"What makes you think this?" Chama asked.

"I don't trust Major Willoughby. He's in charge, but someone inside that fort had to tell Ferguson where O'Hara was. It's a big country."

"I see," Chama said. "I wondered about that myself. Whoever took Ted knew where he would be."

"Makes you wonder, doesn't it?"

"Why do you say the name of Ferguson? Is that one of his wagons we are following?"

Zak told Chama about the two soldiers, the coach and Colleen O'Hara, his suspicion that Apaches had not killed the two soldiers. He also told him about the men he had seen at the way stations and what they had told him.

"You know," Chama said, "that there are many whites who want the Chiricahua driven from their lands. They want to kill them or drive them far away."

"I'm beginning to see all that, yes."

"Many white people think that the only good Apache is a dead Apache."

Zak had heard that talk many times before, applied to any red man. It galled him, as it galled Crook, and his blood boiled not only at the blind prejudice of the comment, but because he knew good men and bad of both races, the white and the red. And he knew that the color of a man's skin did not reflect what was inside the man.

"Fear," Zak said.

"What?"

"We fear whatever we don't know, Jimmy. The white man fears the red man because he doesn't know him. And he never will unless he shakes a red man's hand and sits down inside his lodge and takes supper with his family. Same goes for the red man, too, of course."

"I never heard a white man talk the way you do, Cody."

"Maybe that's because I'm a breed," Zak said, "same as you."

"You are of the mixed blood? Apache?"

"No. My mother was Lakota. Of the Ogallala tribe."

Chama looked cockeyed at Zak. "Your Indian blood does not show much."

"Does it matter? Blood is the same in all men. Mine is as red as yours and yours is as red as any white man's."

"That is not what the white men say."

"No, that is true."

Zak let the sadness of his words hang in the air between them. He could almost see the thoughts work through Chama's mind, see it twitch ever so slightly in the muscles on his face. He knew it must have been hard on the young man, growing up with the Mescaleros and trying to find his father's people among the Mexicans, and seeing how they, too, were treated by what the Indians called "the white man." Skin. Like the coat of a horse or a longhorn cow, it came in all colors on a human. Yet men separated themselves according to their outward coloring and believed their blood was different, when in truth it was all the same.

"My uncle," Zak said, "*Tashunka Watogala*, Talking Horse, once told me that truth could not be put into words. He said that all we see with our eyes is not true. Only the things that cannot be seen are real and important."

"Your uncle sounds like a wise man," Chama said.

"He was a wise man. He taught me much. As did my mother, although I did not realize it at the time."

"When we are young, we do not wish to learn from the old ones. But we learn anyway," Chama said. "And when an old man dies, he takes all of his wisdom with him. If we do not listen to his words when he is alive, they are lost forever."

Zak nodded, then shook off the thoughts that came rushing in, the words of Talking Horse, his mother, his own father. Good words. Not the truth, perhaps, but guideposts to the truths that lay hidden in plain sight.

"We're not going to catch that wagon," Zak

said, "but I aim to put these supply stations out of business. You want to ride along?"

"But, of course. I am on the same trail as you, Cody."

"There could be gunplay."

Chama looked down at the pistol strapped to his waist.

"That is why I carry this pistol, Cody. If it is called upon, it will speak."

Zak's mouth curved in a lazy smile.

He turned his horse and set out toward the adobe he had seen in the distance. They followed the wagon tracks, then climbed another hill to survey the trail ahead. The adobe sat atop a rocky knoll, less than a mile distant. Horses milled in a pole corral some yards from the dwelling. Shimmering pools of watery light shone like fallen stars all around, dancing and disappearing with every turn of the head. The light was blinding and Zak did not look at any of the mirages directly, but scanned the adobe for movement, for any sign of life.

"See anything, Chama?"

"A white man will not bask in the sun like a lizard on such a day as this. If a man is there, he is inside, where the adobe is cool."

"He could be watching us."

"No. There is no shadow at the window."

"You have the eyes of an eagle, Chama."

Chama chuckled. "I think that you see as well as I, Cody."

They rode down the slope of the hill, the cobbles clunking under their horses' hooves, tumbling where they were dislodged, rolling a few inches before they halted and lay still once again.

They stayed to the flat, following the wagon ruts. These were crumbling and their edges lost to the wind, but still plainly visible, days old.

"We'd better split up, Chama," Zak said. "Come at the adobe from the sides. I'll ride up in front, call the man out. You can flank me if he opens up on me. Could be more than one man, too."

"We will see," Chama said.

Chama rode off then, on a tangent, making a wide circle so he would come up on another side of the adobe. Zak rode straight toward it, his senses honed to a keen sharpness, alert for any signs of life or belligerence.

He closed to within a hundred yards of the front door, giving Nox his head. He saw his ears stiffen and twist. The horse arched his back, lifted his head high. His neck stiffened.

What was Nox seeing that was not there? Zak wondered.

The horses in the corral spotted him and one of them whickered.

Fifty yards away. No movement at the window. The door was closed tight.

Forty yards and Nox seemed to stiffen all over, step more gingerly. Zak let his right hand fall to his holster. He put a thumb on the hammer of his pistol.

The breeze blew against his face. A small sudden gust whipped him, stung his cheeks with grit.

He thought he heard a metallic sound.

Then he heard the *whump* of a rifle booming from inside the adobe. Instinctively, Zak hunched forward, his body hiding behind Nox's neck.

He heard the whoosh of a bullet, saw it kick

up dust as it plowed a divot ten yards in front of
them.

"You opened the ball, you sonofabitch," Zak said
to himself and drew his pistol as he dug spurs into
Nox's flanks and charged straight at the adobe.

He knew the rifle that the man used, from its
deep-throated roar, muffled by the adobe walls. He
knew just how long it would take for the man to
fire that rifle again, and each second that passed
seemed an eternity.

Life hung on such a slender thread, he thought,
and he could feel that thread stretching, stretching,
to the breaking point.

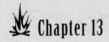 **Chapter 13**

The Big Fifty.

The sound of the Sharps was unmistakable, and Zak knew he had only seconds to get out of the line of fire before the shooter could reload the single shot rifle. He saw the puff of white smoke cloud the window ledge in the lower left-hand corner. He rode hard to come up in front of the house before the man inside could get off a second shot.

Nox's muscles bunched up and he galloped as the energy in those muscles uncoiled. He stretched out his neck and laid his ears down, raced under the guidance of the bit in his teeth.

There was no second shot by the time Zak reached the front of the house. He took Nox around the corner to the other side, jumped out of the saddle and hunched down beneath a window on that side.

The scrape of a boot and Zak whirled, his pistol a part of him, swinging like a weather vane to come to bear on whoever was coming around the corner of the adobe.

Chama stepped into view, hunched over, pistol

in hand. He tiptoed toward Zak, who waved him down even closer to the ground.

"See anything?" Chama said.

Zak shook his head. "What's out back?" he asked.

"A worn-down old wall, a boarded-up window."

The adobe bricks were crumbling, the gypsum almost all washed away, sand along the base of the very old building.

Zak pressed his ear against the wall, listened. He heard only the faint susurrance of the breeze against the eaves and the faint rustle of the nearby brush. Underneath, a silence seemed to find harbor in the adobe wall and within.

"You get hit?" Chama whispered.

Zak pulled away from the wall, shook his head.

"I think there is only one man inside," Chama whispered.

Zak nodded in agreement.

"Jimmy, can you sneak by that front door, go around to the other side, under the open window?"

"Yes, I can do that."

"I'm going to call the man out through the front door. If he doesn't come out, I'll bust in. When you hear that door crash open, you cover that window."

"You will take all the risk, Cody."

"No. It's dark inside. You won't be able to see well through that window, but if he shoots at me, you'll have a shot."

"And you?"

"He might surrender without a fight."

"That would be the smart thing to do."

The two men considered their moves for a moment.

When Chama was ready, he nodded. Zak waved him on past him. Chama crawled on his hands and knees around the front of the adobe. He made no sound, took his time. Zak followed, also on his hands and knees. He stopped on one side of the door as Chama disappeared around the corner of the house.

Zak waited. He put an ear to the door and listened.

He heard the soft sounds, like dream noises from another dimension. The shuffle of a leather sandal sole on dry earth, the faint metallic scrapings as if someone was fiddling with a stuck brass doorknob. Heavy breathing, anxious breathing, like someone gripped with fear and urgency.

Something about those odd confluences of sounds made him think that there was a child or an idiot on the other side of the door, someone confused and in a state of increasing panic. Someone demented and scared, an imbecile who couldn't figure out what to do.

Zak touched a finger to the door, pushed gently. It moved, and the leather hinges made no sound. He pushed with the heel of his hand and the door opened wider, letting a shaft of sunlight pour a sallow streak onto a dirt floor that showed signs that it had been swept flat with a broom. He craned his neck as he brought his pistol up close to the doorjamb, ready to push it through the opening and squeeze the trigger if someone came toward him.

The sounds were louder now. A rustle of cloth, a deep sigh, and that same metallic chitter sounding like a tin grasshopper working its mandibles, or a squirrel muttering low in its mechanical throat.

He saw movement and stretched his neck to look inside toward the window where someone had shot at him moments before.

A dark shape and the unmistakable straight line of a rifle barrel silhouetted against the window's pale light. A figure hunched over, fiddling with the trigger or the trigger guard. The action on the Sharps was jammed, he figured, and the shooter had not ejected the empty hull nor jammed in another .50 caliber round.

Zak eased up through the doorway, still hunched over in a crouch, and stepped carefully onto the dirt floor. He made no sound as he tiptoed toward the figure with its back to him. He knew, from a quick glance, that there was no one else in the room. Just that bent form below the window, struggling with the Sharps, absorbed in freeing the jam, breathing hard and fast, the sucking in and out of an open mouth and nostrils.

Zak grabbed the end of the barrel as he rammed the barrel of his pistol into the back of the person's head. He thumbed the hammer back on the Walker Colt to full cock, the sound like an iron door opening in a dark cave.

"One twitch," Zak said, "and I blow your brains to powder."

He heard a startled gasp that sounded almost like a sob, and he snatched the rifle out of the squatting person's hands, tossed it to the side and behind him.

"Just stand up," Zak said. "Real slow."

He looked downward at long black hair. As the figure rose from the floor, he saw it stream down the back of her dress. He felt something tighten in his throat. A lump began to form as she slowly turned around and looked up at him. Her lips were quivering in fear and her dress rippled from her shaking legs.

"Jimmy," Zak yelled toward the window, "you can come in now."

He saw the crown of Jimmy's hat bob up in the window, then disappear. A moment later Chama entered the hut, pistol in hand.

"Lady," Zak said, "step out where I can see you. We won't hurt you."

She was young, Zak could tell that. But as she stepped toward him, he could see that her eyes were very old, and full of pain, the pain of centuries, and the pain of her present existence. Her brown eyes lay in watery tired sockets and the flesh beneath them was darker than her face, sagging from too many nights of weeping and maybe hard drinking. There was an odd smell in the room, one that he could not define, but was faintly familiar.

Chama walked over to a table and picked up a clay pipe, sniffed it.

"Opium," he said. "She's been smoking opium."

"That's what I smelled," Zak said. "The room reeks with it."

"*Quien eres?*" the woman said in Spanish.

"My name's Cody. Do you speak English?"

"Yes. I speak it."

"What is your name?"

"Her name," Chama said, "is Carmen Delgado. She is the wife of Julio Delgado."

"You know her?"

"I have seen her before," Jimmy said. "In the jail at Taos. She was bailing out her husband, Julio, who had beaten her up the night before."

"Is this true?" Zak asked Carmen.

"He did not mean it. Julio gets loco sometimes. When he drinks too much."

"Julio stole *tiswin* from a Chiricahua and killed the man he stole it from," Chama said. "I tracked him to Taos."

"You didn't arrest him?"

"I tried. Nobody would listen to me. Julio is a bad man, a killer."

Carmen's eyes flashed. "*Mentiroso*," she spat, her eyes blazing. "You liar," she said in English.

"It is true," Chama said. "The Apaches would like to see Julio hanged, or if they could get their hands on him, they would cut him into many pieces."

"Well, Carmen," Zak said, "looks like Julio run off and left you here by yourself."

"He come back," she said.

"Was he one of those who painted himself like an Apache?"

"I no tell you nothing," she said.

Chama stepped in close and glared at her.

"Answer the questions," he said. "Maybe he won't kill you." He spoke in Spanish, but Zak understood every word.

"That's good advice, Carmen," Zak said. "You want to live, don't you?"

She didn't answer.

Zak picked up the clay pipe, held it front of her.

"You want to dream again, don't you?" he said.

Her eyes flashed, burned with need, with longing. Then they returned to their dull dead state as her shoulders slumped. She seemed resigned to the hell she was probably going through, but her lips pressed together in defiance.

"Just tell me their names, Carmen," Zak said, "and you can fill your pipe."

"They are friends of Julio," she said.

"They work for Hiram Ferguson, don't they?"

Her eyes widened and flashed again. "You know they do."

"Tell me their names."

Chama put the snout of his pistol up against Carmen's temple. He thumbed the hammer back. The double click sounded like a lock opening on an iron tomb. Silence filled the room as the blood drained from Carmen's face.

"They have gone," she said. "You will not catch them."

"No matter. But I want to know their names. There were six of them. Julio was one of them."

"Yes," she spat. "Julio is their leader. He is a very strong man. If you go after him, he will kill you."

"The names," Zak said.

Chama pushed the barrel of his pistol hard against Carmen's temple. She winced and licked dry lips with a dry tongue.

"No matter to me," she said. "Hector Gonzalez and his brother, Fidel. Renaldo Valdez, Jaime Elizondo, and Manuel Diego. They ride with Julio." She paused, then said, "Give me the pipe."

Chama eased the hammer down to half cock and pulled the pistol away from Carmen's face. But it still pointed at her.

"I think you've had enough opium, Carmen,"

Zak said. "Now, we're going for a little ride."

"Where do we go?" she said.

"To the next one of these adobe way stations, then to Tucson. To find Julio."

"He will kill you," she said, and as Zak threw the pipe down on the dirt floor, a shadow of a sadness came into her eyes and her dry tongue laved her lower lip.

"Saddle a horse for her, Jimmy, will you? Let's get the hell out of here, out of this stink."

The adobe reeked with the stench of whiskey, opium fumes, stale bread, and moldy tortillas. But there was also the lingering scent of pipe tobacco and burnt powder from the Sharps. Zak picked up the rifle, examined it. There was a dent in the receiver's action, a dimple that kept it from ejecting unless force was used. Apparently, he thought, Carmen didn't have the strength to force the breech open. And she was not even a good shot.

"Why would Julio leave you here all by yourself?" Zak asked her after Chama had taken saddle, bridle, and blanket from a corner and lugged it outside.

"He said he would be back soon."

"What's soon?"

"Two days, he say. Maybe three."

"Do you know why he was coming back?"

"No."

"Who was here before you came? The man who was watching the place, taking care of the stock?"

"I do not know his name. He works for Hiram."

"He went back with the wagon? With the army lieutenant?"

"There was a man in the wagon. His hands and feet were tied with rope. He did not wear an army uniform."

"But you knew he was a soldier?"

Carmen nodded. "They said he was a soldier."

"Do you know where they took this soldier?"

"To Tucson. To the office of Hiram, I think."

"Did Julio ride with the wagon?"

"No. The wagon came after he left."

Zak threw the rifle down. He picked up a lamp, shook it. There was the gurgle of oil inside its base. He pulled the stopper and splashed the coal oil around the room.

"What do you do?" Carmen asked.

"Nobody's going to use this adobe again," he said.

"You burn?"

Zak ushered her to the door, turned and struck a match. He tossed it on a place where the coal oil made a dark stain. The match flared and guttered, then flared again as the heat reached the coal oil. The oil burst into a small flame that grew larger.

"My purse," Carmen said. "My boots."

"Too late," Zak said, stepping outside and closing the door.

Inside, he could hear the crackle of flames as the fire fed on dry wood and cloth. Chama had finished saddling a horse for Carmen. He waited, holding the reins of his horse and the one he had just saddled. Zak whistled and Nox trotted up to him.

Smoke billowed from the adobe as the three rode off. Carmen looked back at the burning adobe, that same flicker of sadness in her eyes that Zak had seen before. Then she turned back around and held her head high, staring straight ahead at Chama, who rode in front, following the wagon tracks.

Zak felt sorry for her. She had nothing, and she had just lost everything.

He knew the feeling.

✸ Chapter 14

Lieutenant Theodore Patrick O'Hara dozed on the bunk, pretending to be in a deep sleep. At least the torture was over for the time being, he thought. A small victory in the early stages of what he expected would be a long battle. Hiram Ferguson had been only a small assault force. Ted knew that he still must face the main battalion, and that was Ben Trask. Trask was the major force, and he was formidable.

Moonlight streamed through the window above Ted's bunk, splashing dappled shadows that flirted with those sprawled by the lamp upon the wooden floor. A column of gauzy light shimmered with dancing dust motes that resembled the ghostly bodies of fireflies whose own lights no longer shone.

He was strapped down to the bunk, one of several in a bunkhouse for the stage drivers. Two were asleep across the room, one of whom was snoring loudly. Watching him was Jesse Bob Cavins, his chair tilted back against the wooden wall under a lighted lamp. He was reading a dime novel, his lips moving soundlessly as he struggled with some of the words.

Ted tested his bonds for the dozenth time, the leather cutting into his wrists, too strong to break. Thoughts of his sister Colleen drifted into his mind unbidden. Guilt-laden thoughts. He never should have suggested to the post commandant, Captain Reuben Bernard, that Colleen be hired to teach the women and children of the Chiricahua tribe. Ted had argued that there would never be peace in Apache land unless the Indians assimilated the English language. Colleen had agreed to come to Fort Bowie. She saw it as a challenge and an opportunity to bring about peace between Cochise and the whites.

Certainly the army had failed, Ted knew.

Captain Bernard, under orders, had waged a fierce and brutal campaign against the Apaches when Ted first came to the fort. He rode with Bernard as he attacked Apache villages, killing eighteen warriors in one, late in 1869. Early the next year, they swarmed down on another village, killing thirteen warriors, and just this year Ted had engaged in another village attack that left nine Apaches dead.

All to no avail, because the Apache war parties increased their depredations, attacking settlements and lone settlers, killing mail carriers and travelers out on the open plain. They even attacked army patrols, as if to show both their defiance and their bravery, and when Bernard sent detachments after the culprits, the soldiers always returned to the post empty-handed and dispirited after fruitless searches over desolate and difficult terrain.

Tom Jeffords had been brought in to palaver

with the Apaches, bring them to the council table, beg them to stop their bloody raids on white villages. Some progress had been made and Bernard sent Ted out under a flag of truce to locate Apache villages and strongholds without engaging any of them in battle. Jeffords had paved the way, and Ted was able to locate many Apache camps. These he marked on a map with a special code. The X's did not denote the location of the actual camps, but denoted a marked spot where Ted had written down numbers that indicated the actual location. These numbers were meaningless to anyone but army personnel.

But Trask did not know that. Not yet. And by now, Ted reasoned, the army would be looking for him. If he could lead Trask and his cohorts on a wild goose chase, sooner or later they would encounter an army patrol and he would be freed. That was his reasoning as he lay there in the dark, thinking of Colleen and his fellow troopers, sweat beading up on his forehead and soaking the skin under his arms and at the small of his back.

He worried about Colleen because now he knew that Ferguson had eyes and ears inside Fort Bowie. That was evident in their threats and their knowledge of troop movements. Ferguson, or Trask, or both, had an informant on the post, either an army man or a civilian. It was disconcerting, but he knew there were soldiers who sympathized with the civilian whites, soldiers who wanted to drive the Apaches from Arizona or tack all their hides to a barn door and set the barn afire.

The motives of such soldiers and the motives of civilians were easy for him to understand. What puzzled him now was the motive of Ben Trask. He had discerned that Trask was in Ferguson's employ, but he also deduced that Trask was not the following kind. He was like a coiled spring, inert for the moment but on the verge of exploding into something entirely different.

What did Trask want?

Ted had a hunch that he would know the answer to that question very soon. Trask was so full of deceit, he reeked with it, like some fakir's woven basket that, when opened, would reveal a writhing nest of snakes within. Trask had something else on his mind besides wiping out Apaches. Ferguson might be under the illusion that Trask was in his employ, but Trask was using Ferguson to achieve his own ends. Ted did not yet know what those ends were, but he'd studied the man enough in the few hours he had been observing him to know that Trask had no ideals, no conscience, no common purpose he shared with Ferguson. He was like a cur, pretending to be friendly and loyal, who at the right moment would snarl and snap and tear a person to pieces with his deadly teeth.

Trask was the man to watch. Ferguson was weak and indecisive. Trask was strong and purposeful, although he concealed from others what he really wanted. He was playing along with Ferguson, but there was no loyalty there, and the pay he got from Ferguson was not compensation enough. And Ted knew that Trask wanted something from him that went beyond the location of Apache camps and strongholds.

Still fresh in his mind was his meeting with the wily and wise Chiricahua leader, Cochise. Tom Jeffords had arranged the meeting, and Ted had to travel without an army escort. It had been just him and Tom, and the ride took nearly two days through rugged country. Tom had apologized when he told him, at the last part of the trip, that he would have to go the rest of the way blindfolded. That was Cochise's wish and there was no negotiating the terms.

Wearing the blindfold, he had ridden with Jeffords up through a steep canyon. Tom told him there were Apaches in the hills watching their progress, that they all had rifles and were within easy range.

"I can't tell you much more than that, Ted, sorry. But you have a right to know what kind of country we're in. Even if you rode up here without a blindfold, you'd never find your way back."

"I guess I have to trust you, Tom. And Cochise, too."

"Cochise is a man of his word. You will come to no harm while you're with me."

Ted was thoroughly confused by the time they halted in Cochise's camp. When Tom took off his blindfold, the glare of the sun blinded him for several seconds. Then he knew he was looking into the eyes of Cochise, looking into centuries of warfare, blood and pain, and he saw mystic shadows in Cochise's eyes, a knowing that was almost beyond human comprehension.

He was a small, wiry man, with a rugged moon face lined with deep weathered fissures. He looked, Ted thought, like a wounded eagle that was still full of fight. He wore a loose-fitting muslin shirt and a colored bolt of cloth wrapped around his head,

his graying hair spiking from it like weathered
splinters of wood. He wore a pistol and knife. A
rifle and bandoleros sat nearby, within easy reach.
Ponies stood at every lean-to, hip-shot, switching
their tails at flies, their eyelids drooping like leather
cowls on hunting hawks.

Apache men sat under lean-to structures made of
sticks and stones that stood against canyon walls.
They were little more than temporary shelters,
and blended into the terrain, forming no discern-
ible pattern. There were no women or children
that Ted could see, and he knew he was in a war
camp. Armed Apaches stood on rocky lookouts
high above them, or sat, half hidden, squatted in
clumps of cactus and stones, barely visible, their
rifles and bandoleros glinting in the sun. The fire
rings were under latticed roofs that broke up the
smoke when it rose so that no sign of their presence ever reached the sky above the hills. It smelled
of cooked meat and the dung of horses and men. It
smelled of sand and rock and cactus blooms.

"You sit," Cochise said in English. "We smoke."

Ted smoked with the Apache chieftain, while
Apache braves sat around them in a half circle,
their faces stoical as stone, their eyes glittering like
polished obsidian beads. He and Cochise talked,
and Cochise asked and answered questions, as he
did, too.

"Did you kill Apaches when you rode with the
white eyes, Captain?" Cochise asked.

"Yes."

"Did you kill women?"

"No."

"My children?"

"No," Ted answered.

Then he asked Cochise: "Have you killed white men?"

"Yes," Cochise said.

"The army does not want to keep fighting the Chiricahua. But it does not want the Chiricahua to kill any more white people. The army thinks the two tribes can live together, in peace."

"The white man wants all the land," Cochise said. "Land that the Great Spirit gave to the Chiricahua."

"No, we do not want all your land."

"It is not our land. It belongs to the Great Spirit. He lets us hunt it and live on it and wants us to defend it. The white man drives wooden stakes in the ground and writes words on paper that tell us the land belongs to him."

Ted looked at Jeffords for help.

"That is the white man's way," Jeffords said. "The army wants to protect the Chiricahua and let Cochise have his land. He will keep the white man away from Chiricahua land. That is the white chief's promise to the Chiricahua."

"Is this true?" Cochise asked O'Hara.

"Yes," Ted said.

Before he left the camp, Ted saw a strange sight and it startled him. A white man, dressed in black and riding a black horse, appeared from behind a low hill with two Chiricahua braves. He waved to Cochise, turned his horse and rode off into the hills and canyons that formed a maze around the Apache camp.

Cochise waved back to the man.

"Who was that?" Ted asked without thinking. Jeffords shot him a look of warning.

Cochise caught the look and waved a hand in the air as if to dismiss Jeffords's attempt to silence Ted.

"He is called the Shadow Rider," Cochise said. "He comes to us from the north and he brings the words of the white chief Crook with him. He speaks our tongue."

"But he's a white man," Ted blurted out, still puzzled by the man he had seen.

Cochise shrugged and some shadow of a smile flickered from his leathery face.

"Who is to know what blood runs in the Shadow Rider's veins?" Cochise said. "My people trust him. I trust him."

"Will you also trust this man?" Jeffords asked, nodding toward Ted.

"I think this man speaks with a straight tongue. We will talk about him when you have gone. We will seek wisdom from our elders and from the Great Spirit."

"That is good enough," Jeffords said.

Ted's memory of that strange meeting was still vivid in his mind. He had a great deal of respect for Cochise, and after he reported his visit to Captain Bernard, he felt that peace with the Apaches was possible. He just hoped his superiors felt the same.

He had not told Bernard about the Shadow Rider, but he had asked Jeffords if he knew the man.

"Yes."

"What's his name?"

"Zak Cody," Jeffords told him. "And he is under orders from General Crook."

"Army?"

"I don't know. Once, I think. You better just forget you ever saw him in Cochise's camp. I think he's under secret orders from Crook and from President Grant."

Ted had let out a low whistle of surprise. Though he wanted to know more about Zak Cody and his mission, he'd asked no more questions of Jeffords.

Now, Ted opened one eye and stared at Cavins, then shifted his gaze to the shaft of moonlight streaming through the window. The light seemed placid and steady, but it was swirling with dust motes and air, and when he shifted focus, he could see only the light itself. But when he refocused, the motes twirled like tiny dervishes gone mad, with no apparent pattern to their movements. In that moment before he closed his eyes, he compared the vision to Trask's incomprehensible mind. Somewhere in that brain of his, Trask was scheming and planning.

Ted vowed that he would be patient and learn that secret. He just hoped that he would live that long and beyond that discovery. Trask was a dangerous man, and cunning, as a wolf or a fox is cunning, and he knew he must be careful. Very careful.

Finally, he fell into a restless sleep, dreamless except for shadowy shapes that flitted through the darkness of his mind, indefinable, featureless as dark smoke in a darkened room.

He was awakened by the sound of boots stalking across the floor, and when he opened his eyes, he saw a man shaking one of the stage drivers.

"Time to get up, Cooper," a voice said, and the bearded man on the bunk rose up and rubbed his eyes.

"Shit," the driver said, "it's dark as a well-digger's ass."

"And you got a run to Yuma, Dave."

Cavins had fallen asleep in his tilted chair and he blinked in the low light from the lamp over his head. His paper book had fallen to the floor and lay there like a collapsed tent, open to the page he'd been reading.

Outside, Ted heard the creak and jingle of harness, the snorting of horses, and the low, gravelly voices of men speaking both Spanish and English. The moon had set, or had drifted beyond the window over his bunk. His back was soaked with sweat and his flesh itched under the leather straps.

Trask entered the bunkhouse.

"Cavins, go get some grub," he said.

The other driver woke up, adjusted his suspenders and walked outside to visit the privy. Trask and Ted were alone in the room.

"We'll get those straps off you pretty soon, O'Hara."

Ted just glared at him.

Trask smiled.

"We're going to use your map today. You're going to take us to those places you marked."

"Apaches move around a lot," Ted said. "They could all be gone by now."

"That would be your tough luck, Lieutenant. But I want to ask you something, and it's just between you and me, okay?"

Trask picked up a chair and set it by Ted's bunk. He sat down and leaned over so his voice would not carry.

"Go ahead, Trask. You have me where you want me."

"Patience, patience. Only a little while longer. We'll get some breakfast for you, some hot coffee and you'll be good as new."

Ted sighed, resigned to being bound awhile longer.

"What do you want to know?" he asked Trask.

"When you and your company were checking on the Apaches out there, did you find out where they keep their gold?"

Ted stiffened. "Gold?"

"Yeah. We know they been hiding it somewheres. You must know where they keep it. You tell me."

Now he knew what Trask was really after. Apache gold. There had been rumors of it at the post and in Tucson. He'd never paid much attention to the talk. But now he knew that Trask believed the rumors and he wanted what he thought the Apaches had.

He also knew that his life depended upon his answer to Trask.

He felt as if he were in a roomful of hen's eggs, and if he made a wrong step, he would break those eggs and Trask would have no further use for him. He let the answer form in his mind, take shape, harden into what had to sound like truth coming from his mouth.

Trask's breath blew against his face, hot and smelling of stale whiskey and strong tobacco.

Ted closed his eyes and opened them again.

Trask was still there, leaning close to him, waiting for his answer.

And Ted's throat was full of gravel, and his gut had tightened with fear and uncertainty.

Trask waited for his answer, a cold look in his pale, steely eyes.

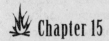 **Chapter 15**

Cloud shadows grazed across the land like the lingering and bewildered shades of sheep. Buttes and mesas stood like the hulks of rusting ships lost on a long ago sea, and the sun blazed down on it all with an unrelenting fire that would bake a lizard's blood. Carmen's face sweated under the brim of her straw hat and no amount of fanning with her hands would push cool air through her mouth and nostrils.

The wagon tracks were dim now, but still visible on the baked sand, like snake tracks turned to fossilized impressions by centuries of sun compacted into a single searing moment. Chama sniffed the air as if seeking a vagrant breeze that might cool his face, dry the sweat soaking from his hairline into his eyes and staining his shirt under his armpits.

Zak worried a small pebble in his mouth, spat it out as he rode up alongside Carmen, who was riding between the two men, Jimmy in the lead, Zak following in the rear.

"You've been to the next station," he said to her. "Know who's there?"

"Why should I tell you anything, gringo?"

"Because I asked you with politeness, Carmen."

"Phaa," she spit, but she could not produce a drop of saliva. "You take me prisoner, make me ride in the hot sun, and you say you are polite? You are *ladrón*, a thief. My husband will kill you as he would kill a cockroach."

"So much killing," he said, half to himself.

"Yes. You. You kill. *Cabrón.*"

"*Verdad*," he said. "True."

"And so, you too will die. By the gun."

"I knew a man," Zak said, "who taught me much. He was a Lakota. An Ogallala."

"I do not know what that is. *Indio?*"

"Yes. He was an Indian. His name was Two Hawks. We were watching the dances. He told me that when the people danced, they held hands. They formed a circle. He said that was to show that all people are connected to one another. That we are all the same, in spirit."

"We are not all the same. I am Mexican. You are gringo, *norteamericano*," she spat as if the very words left a bad taste in her mouth.

Zak looked at her and felt pity.

In her eyes, and in the lines on her face, he saw centuries of suffering and pain. He saw the Yaqui blood beneath the skin on her cheekbones, the faint glow of vermillion smeared across the high planes, the ancient bronze of Moorish ancestors in the cast of her jaw, and the black coals of Spanish mothers so sad and haunting in her eyes.

He thought that she must have been pretty once, as a girl is pretty. With a sweet, smiling face, good white teeth, soft locks of shiny black hair. Now, the years had taken their toll. She was no longer a pretty young girl. But she was a beautiful woman, in the way that old, polished wood is beautiful, in the way a gnarled, wind-blasted tree on the seacoast is beautiful.

"You have the Indian blood in you?" she said after a while. "You do not look it."

"Yes."

"Your mother?"

"Yes."

"But not full blood?"

"No, not full blood," he said.

"That is why you do not show the Indian face of your mother," she said, and he wondered what she was thinking, through that labyrinth her reasoning took her from, that simple black and white place she had come from long ago and journeyed through over so many years.

"Do we ever know who we truly are?" Zak said. "Do we know our fathers and mothers? Can we trace their bloodlines in ourselves? Or do we forge ourselves in their molds so that we look and act the same? If so, that is very sad, and it makes the world a sad place to live."

"The world is a sad place to live," she said, so softly he had to strain to hear it.

"Someday, maybe, if the world keeps growing as it is, as people mingle and marry and leave children to grow, we will all have the same bloodlines. As it was in the beginning."

"The beginning?" she asked querulously, as if she was lost in the fabric of that world he was weaving with his words.

"Adam and Eve."

"The first man and woman," she said.

"Yes. We all sprung from that same seed. Or so the Bible says."

"I do not believe that. We are not all from the same seed. That seed did not carry the blood of blacks and red men and Chinese."

"Skin colors do not matter. A man bleeds the same red blood, no matter the color of his skin."

"Inside, you mean? We are all the same?"

"Yes. Maybe."

"It does not matter to me. I do not think of such things. I know who I am. I know where I came from."

"But do you know where you are going?" he asked, and the question went unanswered as Carmen drew back into herself and wended her way through that labyrinth of reasoning, that maze of bewilderment that faced each person who tried to plumb the depths of life's true meaning.

"You could save some lives if you tell me how many men are at the next station and, maybe, what kind of men they are. We could spare their lives if they have wives and children and just want to ride on instead of fighting us."

"I might tell you who is there," she said, sounding almost like a pouting child.

"I wish you would. Before we get there. Otherwise, we have to assume they will not ride away and we will have to kill them."

"They are just men. They work for Ferguson, too." She paused. "Like my husband."

"Do you know these men?"

"I know their names. They are—"

She broke off and he wondered what she had been going to say. He could see that she was troubled by his questions, by her thoughts about the two men manning the line shack, the way station. Perhaps, he thought, she was worried about her husband as well.

"Are you Catholic?" she asked.

"No."

"I am Catholic. So is my husband. The two men at the little post house are, how do you call them, heathens?"

"They do not believe in God?"

"They believe in money. They bring death with them. That is why they work for Ferguson."

Her words were laden with a sudden bitterness. He sensed that she wished things were different. That her husband did not work for Ferguson, that he did not mingle with such as those two he would soon have to face.

"You do not like Ferguson?" he asked.

She spat. "Filth. Greed. That is what he is. I do not like him."

Zak let out a breath. "These men . . . they are gunmen?"

"Yes. They carry guns. I have heard my husband speak of them. They are robbers. Murderers. These are the kinds of men Ferguson hired to drive away the Chiricahuas. Bad men."

"You do not want this?"

"I do not care," she said. "Nor does my husband. He does not care about Indians, and neither do I."

But she did care. He knew that. Her voice quavered when she spoke of them, and he sensed that she was a dam about to break. She had been alone for a while. With only her thoughts. Now, she had someone to talk to about things she held inside. But he would not draw them out. It would be like lighting a fuse on a stick of dynamite.

"How far to the line shack?" he asked, more to change the subject than to garner information.

She looked around. For landmarks, he thought. Then she looked at the wagon tracks, what was left of an old stage road, as if trying to recall memorable features.

"I know there is more distance between the next one than between all the others. My husband told me this. We will not reach it while the sun is still shining. It will be dark by the time we get to it."

"How do you know this?"

"Because when we left that station, it was dark when we arrived at the other, where Julio left me."

"Then it will be dark," he said. "And maybe that is a good thing."

"You will sneak up on them," she said.

"I will talk to them. If you will tell me their names."

"You want to know who you kill."

Stubborn, she was. Honing in on his words like some bird of prey, pouncing on them with a sharp beak, trying to rip them to shreds.

"So I can call them out. Reason with them."

"To do what?"

"To leave that place without shedding blood."

She uttered a wry laugh, a mirthless laugh that was like the crackle of dried corn husks.

"They are called Lester Cunningham, he is the

oldest, and Dave Newton. Dave has the hot head, how you say it, and Lester, he is the quiet mean one, who is always thinking, who always undresses me with his eyes to make me naked in his mind. Julio does not like him. He does not trust him."

"And this David, your husband trusts him?"

"No, but Julio says he is like the cocked pistol with the hair trigger. *Muy peligroso.*"

"Very dangerous, yes."

They rode on as the sun fell away in the sky, burning into their eyes, and they had cold tamales she had made when they stopped at a small spring just off the wagon path. Zak complimented Carmen on her cooking, even though the meat was old and tough, the cornmeal too salty.

Jimmy Chama had been quiet during the meal, but now, as he sat in the shade of his horse's belly, he spoke to Zak.

"I heard you talking with Carmen," he said. "We will reach the way station after dark."

"Yes."

"What will you do?"

"I will talk to the two men there, tell them to go back to Tucson or die."

"You want me to back you, then. And who will watch Carmen?"

"No, you watch Carmen. And wait. I will talk to them. See if they listen to reason."

Carmen laughed that dry toneless laugh of hers, that scoffing laugh that was at once a sign of wisdom and disbelief.

An old wooden stock tank, the tar in its seams badly shrunk and deteriorated, sat on decaying four-by-four whipsawed beams, the water inside, at the bottom, scummed over with green algae. A lizard lay along the top board, blinking its eyes, wondering if it should venture down into the tank. Zak watched it, knowing that the creature would probably drown if it ventured down to the stagnant water. Flies buzzed around the tank in aimless patterns, rejecting the lizard as a source of food.

"That Lester," she said, "he is always looking. He will see you, or hear you, and then his gun will talk to you. His gun does not reason."

"She's probably right," Chama said. "You will go up against two men. If one doesn't get you, the other one will."

"Yes," Carmen said, her breath hissing over the sibilant like a prowling serpent.

Zak drew a breath.

"I will have the night," he said. "Before the moon is up. I will be only another shadow in the darkness. They'll hear my voice, but they won't see me."

"Ah," Chama said. "You will be the shadow, eh. Is that why you are called *Jinete de Sombra*, the Shadow Rider?"

Zak did not answer.

Carmen looked at Zak, shaken by Chama's question. As if she knew. As if she had heard the appellation before, somewhere. She ate the last of her tamale and washed it down with water, her throat suddenly dry and clogged with meat and masa flour.

Zak looked up at the sky and the puffs of clouds.

The sun had coursed lower on the horizon and would soon set, drawing the long shadows of afternoon into a solid mass, like a burial shroud.

Then the night would come, and he would find out if words would work better than bullets.

Chapter 16

Colleen fanned herself as she faced the class of Chiricahua children and their mothers. She had a large chalkboard to work with, and some children were forced to share their slates with those who had none. It was cooler in the adobe room than outside but still unbearably hot, and she felt the uncomfortable seep of perspiration under her armpits, on the inside of her legs, and beneath her breasts.

She used pictographs to illustrate the English words while she voiced the equivalent in their language, Apache.

"*Ndeen,*'" she said. Man. The children laughed at her stick figures, and sometimes the women did, too.

She taught them to count to five in English, using her fingers.

"*Dalaa, naki, taagi,*'" she would say. One, two, three.

Some of the words were difficult to say, and the children would correct her. Or if they were not sure, one of the mothers would speak up in a loud, gravelly voice and correct her pronunciation.

Colleen had an interpreter, a small, moon-faced

woman named *Tu Litsog,* or Yellow Water. She relied on Yellow Water to convey her teachings.

"The key to language," she said, "is writing. If you make the marks on paper, others can read it. You can send this paper, or carry it, over long distances so that others will know your words."

The children and the women all had pieces of paper and pencils. They all seemed fascinated with the process, and though some made drawings or just meaningless scrawls, by the second day Colleen had them writing down the letters of simple words, like dog, cat, and bird. She was delighted at the response.

"I may be going away, Yellow Water, so do you think you can teach your people to read and write with the materials I will leave with you?"

"I do not know," Yellow Water said.

"They all want to learn."

"I know. They respect the white lady. To them, I am a . . . a turn cloth."

"A turncoat? A traitor?"

"Yes, that is the word. A turncoat, a turn face, I think."

"You must not let that matter. You must teach these children and their mothers. I will return."

"Where do you go?"

"I must find my brother," Colleen said.

There was always a soldier guarding the door, usually a private or a corporal, but a grizzled old sergeant often stopped by to check on the trooper and Colleen. She noticed him and liked him. He seemed to like her as well.

His name was Francis Xavier Toole, and he had been in the army for almost thirty years.

"Francis," she said to him after they had become friends, "why is it necessary to put a guard on these children and women?"

"Oh, ma'am, the guard is not here to watch over the squaws and kiddies, oh no. Major Willoughby has the lads keepin' an eye on yourself."

"On me? Why?"

Toole shrugged, but she knew it was not because he didn't know.

"Be honest with me, Francis," she said. "Why does Major Willoughby think that I need an armed soldier watching me teach children to read and write English?"

"Well, mum, it's not for me to say." He shifted his feet and looked down at them, much like a truant boy might behave when speaking to an inquisitive teacher.

Something was wrong at Fort Bowie—she had known it from the very first day—and when news of her brother's abduction became known to her, and Willoughby or anyone else would not tell her anything, she began to feel shut out. Now, after four days of talking with Toole and asking questions of him, she knew he was struggling with his obligation to the military and his friendship with her. But she was determined to persist.

"Francis, I know you're bound by duty, but I must find out what's happened to my brother. And, somehow, I think Major Willoughby knows more than he's telling. This fort seems to be divided and without a real leader."

"Yes'm," Toole said, shuffling his feet and staring down at them, feeling awkward, and perhaps, she thought, a little ashamed.

"Are you agreeing with me, Francis? Or just being polite?"

"Both, maybe. Major Willoughby is temporary commander of the post, ma'am."

"Until when?"

"I don't know, ma'am."

"But you know he's doing things he should not be doing."

"Ma'am, I'm not privileged to read the major's mind."

"Is he doing anything about finding my brother, Lieutenant Ted O'Hara?"

"I don't know, ma'am."

"Will you please call me Colleen and don't be so stiff and formal with me, Francis."

"Yes'm."

"There you go," she said. "Being polite and proper. And you, with so much wisdom, so much information inside you. Information I may need. As a friend."

She was pressing Francis, she knew. Her face glowed in the wash of the afternoon sunlight, her cheeks painted in soft pastels with the complexion of peaches, her eyes narrowed to block the glare of the sun. Francis looked at her, his lips quivering as if he were boiling over to speak, to divulge what he knew, what he suspected.

"There's only so much I can say, Colleen. Only so much I really know."

"Anything might help," she said. "In either category."

"You mean you want me to speculate?"

"That would be a welcome change from the silence, Francis."

"You push real hard, Colleen. I've seen mules less stubborn. Not to compare you to a mule, mind you . . ."

"Let's not just chat with one another, Francis."

"Well, um, they's some soldiers what want the Apaches done in with. Rubbed out. Same as in town, over to Tucson. Your brother was sent out to locate hostiles, er, I mean, Apaches, and report back to Major Willoughby. I reckon I can speculate that the major might have a reason to do this."

"Yes. I can follow you."

"The major can't do this right out in the open. We're supposed to keep the peace, protect the citizenry of the territory, and help Mr. Jeffords bring Cochise and all the Chiricahuas to the peace table."

"But Willoughby doesn't want this to happen?" she said.

"I don't rightly know."

"Yes, you do. What about my brother? Why was he kidnapped and where was he taken?"

"I figure that faction in Tucson, them men, er, ah, those men, don't want Cochise to get off scot-free. They want him and all the other Apaches made into good Apaches."

"What does that mean?"

"It means dead, Colleen. A good Apache, they say, is a dead Apache."

"And my brother? Was he taken away so that the people in Tucson could kill Cochise? Could murder Apaches?"

"Maybe."

"And who was behind his kidnapping?"

"Same outfit that brung you—I mean brought you—here to Fort Bowie," he said.

"Hiram Ferguson?"

"Yes'm. I reckon."

"You know, you mean."

"My best guess," he said.

"I'm going there," she said.

"Going where?"

"To Hiram Ferguson's. I want to ask him what he did with Ted."

"That could be dangerous, Miss Colleen. Ferguson is one of them drum beaters what wants to wipe out the whole Apache nation. He's got him almost a regular army, I hear tell."

"I'm not afraid of him." But her dimples twittered silently like little bird mouths, quivering at the edge of her nervous, brave smile.

"You can't do nothing, even if Ferguson is behind your brother's kidnap. I mean he won't tell you nothin'. And them layabouts he hires on would just as soon kill you as look at you."

"Will you help me, Francis?"

"Help you? How?"

"I want a horse and a pistol and food to carry me to Tucson. I want to leave tonight. I can't do it without your assistance."

"Ma'am—I mean Colleen—you're askin' a lot. I could stand before a court-martial if I gave you an army horse, let alone a firearm."

"But you'll do it, won't you, Francis?"

Her smile this time was full and warm, a knowing siren's smile, as old as time, a smile that made creases in her dimples, made them wink like con-spiratorial smiles.

"Well, you can't go to Tucson all by yourself, you know."

"Oh, Francis, I can do anything I set my mind to."

"Yes'm, I reckon you can. Matter of fact, a couple of the boys got leave coming and they're riding into Tucson town tonight. Good boys. They could escort you, I reckon."

She smiled again. "Yes, I reckon they could. That would be quite nice, Francis."

"Can you handle a gun? I mean a big old pistol with a kick like a mule?"

"You bet I can, Francis. Ted taught me to shoot, and I can take a pistol apart and clean it and load a cap and ball with nothing more than powder, ball, and spit."

Francis laughed. "All right. You got to be sneaky, though. I'll tell the boys to meet you behind the livery after dark. They won't like waitin' that long to get off to Tucson, but they'll mind what I tell 'em. You'll have a horse waiting there and grub in your saddlebags, a canteen hanging from the horn. Those boys are privates, but they're seasoned. Likable. One of 'em's named Delbert Scofield, the other'n is called Hugo Rivers. They know the way, even in the dark, and they'll give a good account of themselves if you should run into trouble."

"And a big pistol? Ammunition."

"Yes," he said, with a downtrodden tone of sur-render. "All you need. You might want to take something else with you, though, you bein' Irish and all like me."

"What's that, Francis?"

"A four-leaf clover and a St. Chris medal."

"Why, Francis," she said, "I didn't know you cared."

He smiled wanly, then left her standing in the doorway of her schoolhouse.

Colleen watched him walk across the compound, into the sunlight, and she brushed back a strand of copper hair that had fallen over her eyes.

"I'm coming, Ted," she breathed. "I'll find you."

And her voice carried the petulance of a prayer. She hoped she would find Ted alive.

She was prepared to face Ferguson and find out the truth about her brother's kidnapping, where he was.

She would not hesitate to shoot Ferguson or anybody else who got in her way.

And she would shoot to kill.

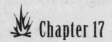 **Chapter 17**

In the distance, across the eerie nightscape of the desert, the yellow light flickered like a winking firefly as they rode through and over small rocky hillocks dotted with the twisted forms of ocotillo and prickly pear. In the darkness, distances were deceiving, but Zak had learned to gauge them through long experience of riding at night in country more deceptive than this.

He left Chama and Carmen behind a low hill above the adobe cabin, out of harm's way, after whispering to Carmen to be quiet. She was skittery, and he had a hunch she might try to warn the two men in the hut. He also told Chama to keep a close eye on her.

"Brain her if you have to, Jimmy," Zak said.

In the darkness, he could see Chama nod.

He circled the lighted shack, a slow process because he didn't want Nox's iron shoes ringing on stone or cracking brush. Through a side window he saw shadows moving inside. The horses in the corral were feeding, so he judged that one of the men, or both, had recently set out hay or grain for them. He patted Nox's withers to calm him, keep him quiet as he neared the end of his wide circle.

Zak dismounted, looped the reins through the saddle rings so they wouldn't dangle, leaving Nox to roam free. The horse would not roam, he knew, but stay within a few feet of where he would leave him, waiting patiently for his master to return. He patted Nox on the neck and walked toward the adobe, his boots making no sound on the hard ground.

He crept up to the edge of the light from one window to the side of the front door. The feeble glow from the lamp puddled on the ground outside, its beam awash with winged gnats flying aimless circuits like demented swimmers. A faint aroma drifted from the window and the cracks around the weathered door that had shrunk with age. Zak sniffed, smelling the distinct aroma of Arbuckle's Best, with its faint scent of cinnamon. He listened, heard the burbling of what he imagined must be a coffeepot on a stove. His stomach swirled and his mouth filled with the seep of saliva.

He loosened his pistol in its holster, stepped up to the door and gave a soft knock.

"Who the hell is it?" growled a voice inside.

"I smell coffee," Zak said. "Lost my horse."

Whispers from inside the adobe. A scuffling of feet, scrape of chairs.

Zak left himself room to step aside if anyone came at him with a gun or a knife.

"Hold on," another voice called out.

The door opened.

Two men stood there, back-lighted, and Zak

couldn't see their faces well. They wore grimy work clothes and their boots had no shine, dust-covered as they were.

"You what?" the taller man in front growled.

"Lost my horse. Well, he broke his leg in a gopher hole and I had to put him down. Been walking for a couple of hours. Saw your light. Smelled that Arbuckle's when I came up."

"Who the hell are you?"

"Name's Jake," Zak said, the lie coming easily to his lips. "Jake Baldwin." A name out of the past, one of the mountain men who had trapped the Rockies with his father. Jake wouldn't mind. He was long dead, his scalp hanging in a Crow lodge up in Montana Territory.

"Let him in, Lester. Jesus."

"Yeah," Lester said. "Come on in. Coffee's just made."

Zak noticed that Lester's dangling right hand was never very far from the butt of his pistol, a Colt Dragoon, from the looks of it. Well worn, too. There was the smell of rotten flesh and decayed fat in the room, mixed with the scent of candle wax and whiskey fumes.

"I'm Dave Newton," the second man said. "We don't get many folks passin' this way, stranger."

"Jake," Zak said, stepping inside where the musty smell of an old dwelling mingled with the scent of the coffee. "Pleased to meet you."

"That's Lester Cunningham," Newton said. "My partner."

"Set down," Cunningham said, his gravelly voice so distinctive that Zak looked at his throat, saw the heavy braid of a scar there, dissecting his Adam's apple. He was a tall, rangy man with long hair the color of steel that hung down past his shirt collar. His complexion was almost as gray, pasty, as if he had been in a prison cell for a good long while.

Newton was a stringy, unkempt man with a sallow complexion, bad teeth, and a strong smell that emanated from his mouth. His scraggly hair stuck out in spikes under his hat, which, like him, had seen better days. His eyes appeared to be crossed, they were so close-set, straddling a thin, bent nose that furthered the illusion. His face and wrists were marbled with pale liver spots, and Zak could see the blue veins in his nose, just under the skin.

As Lester took the coffeepot off the small square woodstove with its rusty chimney, Zak glanced around the room. There were coyote skins drying on withes, others, stiff and stacked, tied into bundles with twine, and, in a small oblong box resembling a cage, a jackrabbit hunched, its eyes glittering with fear. Some potato peelings littered its cage.

Newton saw Zak looking at the rabbit and let out a small chuckle.

"That's Bertie," he said. "Me 'n' Lester pass the time huntin' coyotes at night. We take Bertie out there in the dark and twist his ears till he squeals like a little gal. Them coyotes come slinkin' up for a meal and we pop 'em with our pistols. For sport. But we can sell them hides to the Mexicans in Tucson for two bits or so. Drinkin' money."

Zak saw that both men wore skinning knives on their belts. Newton packed an old Navy Colt, converted from percussion to handle cartridges. The brass on it was as mottled as his skin.

Lester poured coffee into three grimy cups. He handed one to Zak, who took it in his left hand, the steam curling up from its surface like tiny wisps of fog.

"What's this about your horse?" Cunningham asked. "You say it stepped in a gopher hole? I ain't seen no gophers 'round here."

"It was a hole," Zak said. "I thought it was a gopher hole. Maybe a prairie dog hole."

He held the cup up to his lips, blew on it, but he didn't drink.

"Ain't seen no prairie dogs 'round here neither," Cunningham said. "Where'd you say you was from?"

"I didn't say," Zak said.

"Les, you don't need to be so unsociable," Newton said. "Let the man drink his coffee."

"He ain't drinkin' none," Cunningham said. "You left-handed, mister?"

"I'm ambidextrous," Zak said.

"Huh?" Newton said.

"Yeah, what's that?" Cunningham said. "Some kind of disease? That abmi—whatever."

"Ambidextrous. Means I'm good with either hand, Lester," Zak said, an amiable tone in his voice. "From the Latin. 'Ambi' means both. 'Dextrous' means right."

Both men worried over Zak's explanation. Newton was the first to figure it out.

"That means you got two right hands?"

"Something like that," Zak said. "Means I can write or play with my pecker using either hand."

Newton laughed. Cunningham scowled.

"Mister, seems to me you got a smart mouth,"

Cunningham said. "Something wrong with the coffee?"

"No, why?" Zak said.

"You ain't drinkin' it."

"Too hot."

"How come you're holding that cup with your left hand?" Cunningham said.

"Oh, it was the handiest, I reckon," Zak said with a disingenuous smile.

"Or maybe you mean to draw that Walker and rob us," Cunningham said.

"You got something to rob?"

Newton chuckled. "He's got you there, Les," he said.

"I don't like the bastard," Cunningham said. "We don't know where he come from. We don't know what he wants. He asks for coffee, then don't drink it. Shit, he's got something up his damned sleeve besides an arm."

"Aw, Les, you go on too much about nothin'," Newton said. "Coffee's real hot. He don't want to burn his lips."

Zak looked at the two men. Newton was oblivious to the threat voiced by Cunningham, or was unaware of the tension between the two men. But he wasn't. Cunningham's eyes were narrowed to slits and he looked like a puma ready to pounce. He decided he had played with them long enough.

He set his coffee cup down on the floor. Cunningham's gaze followed it and he stiffened. Newton looked like an idiot that had just seen a parlor trick he didn't understand.

But Zak noticed that Newton was wearing a swivel holster. He wouldn't even have to draw his pistol, just reach down, cock it as he brought the holster up on the swivel, then fire. Of the two men in the adobe, Zak figured Newton was the more dangerous one, even though he showed no signs of being belligerent.

It was the quiet ones you had to watch, he thought.

"I don't know," Zak said softly, shaking his head, "he must have scraped the bottom of the barrel."

"What's that?" Cunningham said. "Who you talkin' about?"

"Old Hiram," Zak said.

"Hiram?" Newton came out of his seeming stupor at the mention of the name.

"Ferguson?" Cunningham said. "You talkin' 'bout Hiram Ferguson?"

"Yeah, that's the man," Zak said.

"You work for him?" Newton asked, an idiotic expression on his face.

"Nope," Zak said.

"What's that about scrapin' the bottom of the barrel?" Cunningham said, pressing the issue.

"When he hired you two on," Zak said.

"What the hell . . ." Newton said, setting his cup down on a small table.

"You got somethin' in your craw, mister, you spit it out." Cunningham's right hand drifted closer to the butt of his pistol.

Zak sensed that both men were ready to open the ball. But he wanted to give them a chance, at least.

"Your other way stations up the line are all shut down," Zak said. "The men manning them are either lighting a shuck for Tucson or wolf meat. You two boys got yourself a choice."

"Yeah, what's that?" Cunningham said, his right hand opening, dropping lower still.

"You can either walk out of here, saddle up and ride back to Tucson, or . . ."

Zak reached down, casually, and picked up his coffee cup. It was still steaming.

"Or what?" Newton said, a menacing tone in his voice that was like a razor scraping on a leather strop.

"Or you'll both be corpses lying here when I burn this shack down," Zak said.

That's when Cunningham made his move. His hand dropped to the butt of his Dragoon. Zak tossed the hot coffee at him. Cunningham screamed and clawed at his face. Then Zak hurled the empty cup straight at Newton and stood up, crouching as his hand streaked for the Walker at his side.

Newton dodged the cup and tilted his holster up, hammering back with pressure from his thumb. Too late. Zak had already jerked his pistol free, cocking on the rise, and squeezed the trigger when the barrel came level with Newton's gut. The pistol roared and bucked in his hand, spewing lead and sparks and flame from its snout like some angry dragon.

Cunningham rose to his feet and drew the big Dragoon from its holster, his eyes blinking at the sting of hot coffee.

Zak swung his pistol and made it bark with another squeeze of the trigger. The bullet smashed into Cunningham's belly and he doubled over with the shock of the impact.

"You drop that pistol, Lester," Zak said, "or the next one goes right between your eyes."

Newton groaned and started to lift his pistol to fire at Zak.

"Don't you get it, Newton?" Zak said. "You just stepped on a rattlesnake."

"Huh?" Newton said, his voice almost a squeak as the pain started to spread through his bowels.

"I'm the rattler," Zak said, and shot again, drilling Newton square in the chest, cracking his breastplate and tearing out a chunk of his heart. There was a gush of blood and Newton dropped like a sack of stones.

Cunningham let his pistol fall and rolled on the floor, his back in the dirt. He stared up at Zak, his eyes glassy from the pain that seeped through him like a slow brushfire.

"Who in the hell are you, mister?" Cunningham managed to say. "We ain't done you no harm."

"It's the Apache you're hurting, Cunningham. I gave you a choice. Go or die. You chose the wrong one."

"How—How many of you are there?" Cunningham said. "You got men outside?"

"There's a nation outside, Lester. A whole nation of Apaches."

"I don't get it," Cunningham said, his voice fading as his eyes began to glaze over with the frost of death.

He shuddered and there was a crackle in his throat. He let out a long sigh and couldn't get any breath back in his lungs. He closed his eyes and went limp.

Zak looked at the two men. Both were dead and there was a silence in the room that was both blessed and cursed.

Zak walked to the cage. He took the cage outside, set it on the ground. He lifted the door, and Bertie hopped out. Zak made a sound to scare the rabbit off, then returned to the shack.

"And you won't kill any more coyotes, either," Zak said as he picked up the oil lamp and hurled it against the wall, hitting it just above the bundle of hides. Tongues of flames leaped in all directions and began licking at the dried fur, anything that would burn.

Zak stepped outside into the clean dry air. He opened the gate to the Colt and started ejecting spent hulls. He stuffed new cartridges into the pistol as he walked slowly toward the place where he had left Nox. Before he mounted up, he could smell the sickly aroma of burning human flesh.

🌵 Chapter 18

Ben Trask cursed the rising sun. He jerked the cinch strap tight, drove a fist into his horse's belly. The horse flinched and drew up its sagging belly, giving Trask another notch on the cinch. He buckled it and turned to the others in the stable.

"Jesse Bob, you and Willy about finished yonder?"

"Just about, Ben," Cavins said, but he was still trying to load his saddle over the blanket. His horse was sidestepping every attempt.

"I got to finish curryin' mine," Rawlins said. "He wallowed in shit durin' the night."

The eastern horizon was a blaze of red, as if billions of sumacs had exploded and dripped crimson leaves in the sky. There was a majesty and an ominous hush across the desert as the sun spread molten copper over the rocks and plants.

"It's goin' to be hotter'n a two-dollar pistol out there today," Trask grumbled. "We should have been gone long before sunrise."

"Nobody woke us up," Cavins complained. "Hell, we even hit the kip with our clothes on last night."

"It's that damned Ferguson," Rawlins said. "He said he'd have somebody wake us up before dawn."

"Where in hell is Ferguson?" Trask said, a nasty snarl in his voice. "It looks like we got a bunch of barn rats in here and no sign of Hiram."

"He said he had business to take care of," Cavins said. "He'll be along directly."

"There's only one business this day. Damn his stage line anyway."

The Mexicans were almost finished saddling their horses and were leading them out of the stables. Ferguson waded through them into the barn and started yelling at Lou Grissom.

"You got my horse saddled yet, Lou?"

"Yes, sir. He's still in his stall, though."

"Shit, you could have brought him out. Ben, this is a hell of a day for whatever you got planned," Ferguson said as he approached Trask.

"Climb down off your high horse, Hiram," Trask said. "You know the stakes."

"No, I don't know the damned stakes. I got one plan, you got another."

"O'Hara's map's gonna lead us right to the head honcho Apache hisself. We can wipe 'em out in one blow. With my men and yours, them what's in those line shacks, we'll have a small army. Just make sure everybody's got plenty of cartridges, and it wouldn't hurt to take along a few sticks of dynamite."

"Christ, Ben, what makes you think you can trust that soldier boy?"

"Did you hear that horse come in early this morning, runnin' like a bat out of hell?"

"Nope. I slept like a dadgummed log all night."

"That was a rider from Fort Bowie. Wore out saddle leather and his horse to bring me a message from Willoughby."

"Yeah?"

"Yeah. O'Hara's baby sister left the fort night before last, headin' straight for your place. I told O'Hara if this didn't pan out, she'd be the first to die, and he could watch her bleed."

"He swallered that?"

"Shivered like a dog shittin' peach seeds," Trask said.

Hiram found that hard to believe. O'Hara hadn't impressed him as a man who was much afraid of anything. But, of course, he would have strong feelings for his sister and might fear that harm would come to her if he didn't cooperate. And he had to admit, Trask was a bear of a man who could easily make most men think twice before bucking him.

"Well, just watch out he don't trick you, Ben. O'Hara looks to me like a man who puts a card or two up his sleeve when he's at the table."

"He won't double-cross us, Hiram. If he does, he's a dead man."

They finished saddling their horses and gathered outside the stables. Cavins brought O'Hara from the office. He was dressed in civilian clothing and he was no longer bound. But Cavins had his pistol out of its holster and leveled on him.

"Ready to ride, Lieutenant?" Trask said, patting his shirt where the map stuck out so O'Hara could see it.

"Yes," O'Hara said. "Under protest."

Trask laughed. "Duly noted," he said in a mocking tone. "Climb aboard that steel-dust gray over there. You'll stand out like a sore thumb." With a wave of his arm, Trask indicated all the other horses, which were sorrels and bays.

"Mount up," Trask ordered the others as O'Hara climbed into the saddle, with Cavins watching his every move. O'Hara was the only one unarmed, and he sighed as he looked at the small army of men surrounding him. He knew that he did not have a friend among them, but his philosophy had always been, "Where there's life, there's hope." He just didn't want to put Colleen in jeopardy. By now he had figured out that Ferguson and Trask both had ties to Fort Bowie. Although they had never mentioned any names, he knew that their influence, or their connections, must reach fairly high.

He didn't know much about Willoughby, hadn't seen that much of the major. But he knew, or suspected, that Willoughby's sympathies might lie with the Apache-haters. It was just a feeling. Nothing he could nail down on a roof of proof.

Ted looked at the bloodred sky of dawn, said to Cavins, "Red sky at morning."

"What's that?" Cavins asked.

"Red sky at morning," Ted said, "sailor take warning."

"Well, you ain't no sailor and we ain't anywhere near the sea."

"Don't have to be, Cavins. That sky dominates the earth."

"Shut up, soldier boy," Cavins said. "You so much as twitch on this ride and I'll blow you plumb out of the saddle."

Ted knew that Cavins wouldn't shoot him, but he

saw no reason to argue the point. He was unarmed
and outnumbered, and this was not the place to
make a stand. But he also knew that the first duty
of a prisoner was to make every attempt to escape.
It had been drilled into him at the military academy,
and that thought had been uppermost in his mind
ever since he was captured in the dead of night.

He looked around. All of the men were looking
at the dawn sky. Ted had never seen a more vivid
sunrise. The color was extravagant, plush bulges
of the reddest red, the color of blood, fresh spilled,
after a hot breeze had stiffened it. Yes, it would
be hot that day, but he knew that in another day
or two all hell would break loose as the sky filled
with black bulging clouds and the wind blew dust
and sand into their eyes just before the torrential
rains hit with a force strong enough to blow a man
out of his saddle. He had seen such storms before,
blown down out of the mountains and onto the
desert. He had seen cattle and men washed away
by flash floods and rivers appear in dry creek beds
that brought walls of water rushing headlong at
better than six or seven feet high and then some.

That sky told Ted that within twenty-four hours
they'd be caught up in a gully washer that would
have these men scrambling for high ground, their
eyes stung by grit and rain, blinded for a time, he
hoped, unable to see more than a foot in front of
their faces, if that. There would be a chance then
for him to ride away from his captors, put distance
between him and them as he made his way back to
the fort. It was a chance. Perhaps the only chance
he'd have. They couldn't make it to the first marks

on his map before they would all be swept up in one hell of a frog-strangler of a storm.

Suddenly, he felt an inner surge of energy as a thought occurred to him. He began to calculate the distance in his mind, the estimated speed of travel with this group of armed killers, and he knew it was possible. Possible to outwit Trask and Ferguson, possible to escape. It was a long shot, to be sure, but he was confident there would be time. Time and opportunity. His nerves would be scraped to a fine razor edge when they reached the place he had in mind, but he could handle that.

All he had to do was wait and bide his time, he thought, as he looked at that rude dawn sky again and smiled inwardly.

"Let's get this outfit moving," Trask yelled, as the Mexicans sat their horses, their gazes still fixed on the eastern horizon. Cavins nodded to O'Hara, who turned his horse toward the main bunch of men.

"O'Hara," Trask said, "you ride with me in front. Cavins, you watch him."

"My men," Ferguson said, "you follow behind Cavins."

"Hiram, come on up. You ride with me, too. We're going to pick up those men you got on station. That should give us enough guns to do what we have to do."

"More'n enough," Hiram said. "Them are all good men. Crack shots."

There was grumbling among some of the men who had stayed too long at the cantina the night before, but Trask got the column moving, and the griping stopped once the small troop made the commitment. The sun rose above the horizon, drawing off the night dew and releasing the dry smell of the earth. The shadows evaporated and the rocks and plants stood out in stark relief, as if carved out of crystal with a razor. A horse farted and some of the men laughed.

"I want you to take us straight to where old Cochise has his gold, O'Hara, you got that?" Trask said.

"It's marked on that map in your pocket, Trask. It's a good two-day ride."

"We'll make it in a day and a half."

O'Hara suppressed a smile. That would be perfect in his estimation.

Trask set a pace that brought more grumbling from the men. The Mexicans kept up, as if to show up the gringos, and the muttering stopped once again.

A half hour later, when the smoke of Tucson was no longer visible behind them, Hiram stood up in the stirrups, peering ahead. He uttered an exclamation that there was no equivalent of in any language.

Trask followed his gaze. Small puffs of dust speared on the horizon, golden in the morning light, almost invisible against the desert hue.

"He's wearin' out saddle leather," Trask said.

"Yeah. He's in a mighty hurry, and ridin' the old trail to them ranches where I've got my men on station."

"One of yours?"

"I don't know yet. He's too far away."

"Well, we'll shorten his distance some," Trask

said. "Let's keep up the pace," he called out to the men behind him.

The oncoming rider closed the distance. He loomed up, madly whipping his horse with his reins, the brim of his hat brushed back by the force of the breeze at his face.

"Damned if that ain't Danny Grubb," Hiram said. "And looky at his horse, all lathered up like a barbershop customer."

Flecks of foam flew off Grubb's horse. Hiram held up his hand as if to stop him before the animal floundered.

Grubb reined in when he was a few yards away, hauling hard on the reins to stop the horse. The horse stiffened its forelegs and pulled up a few feet away, its rubbery nostrils distended, blowing out spray and foam. It heaved its chest in an effort to breathe, then hung its head, tossing its mane.

"Danny, you 'bout to kill that horse," Hiram said. "What in hell's the all-fired rush and where the devil are you bound so early in the mornin'?"

"Boss, he done shot Tolliver. Larry's plumb dead. He didn't have a chance."

"Whoa up, Danny. Take it slow. Who shot Larry?"

"Let me get my breath," Grubb said, wheezing. The rails in his throat rattled like a stand of wind-blown cane.

"Just tell me who killed Tolliver and we'll get him," Hiram said.

"C-Cody," Grubb stammered. "Calls hisself Zak Cody. The Shadow Rider."

Trask's blood seemed to stand still in his veins, then turned cold as ice.

"Cody?" Trask said. "Are you sure?"

"Damned sure." Grubb was breathing hard, but he was more anxious to get his story off his chest than to breathe in more air. "I lit out, then circled back a ways to see where he went."

By then the other riders had crowded around Grubb and encircled him, all listening intently.

He looked over at Julio Delgado.

"He took Carmen, Julio. Seen 'em ridin' off, and there's another feller with him now, I reckon. Don't know him. But he burned down most ever' one of them 'dobes and I know he kilt Cunningham and Newton. It was dark as hell, but I seen that 'dobe burnin' and I crossed nobody's trail gettin' this far. That man Cody's a pure devil. And he's headed this way, near as I can figure."

O'Hara listened to this account and was barely breathing as he mulled it over.

He had been watching Trask the whole time and he had now found another one of the man's weaknesses. Besides a lust for gold, Trask was afraid. Afraid of one man—Zak Cody.

The Shadow Rider.

It was something to keep in mind, and Cody just might turn out to be another ace in the hole.

The eastern sky was a ruddy daub on the horizon. The sun lifted above the earth and the clouds began to fade to a soft salmon color. But the warning was still there. A storm was coming that would turn the hard desert floor to mud.

Trask turned around and looked straight at O'Hara as if he had read his thoughts.

Ted O'Hara smiled, and he saw a sudden flash of anger in Trask's eyes.

Well, Ted thought, now we know each other, don't we, Ben Trask?

Trask turned away, and the moment passed. But now Ted felt that he had the upper hand and Trask had no control over the future. Some of the men Trask had counted on were dead. Julio's wife was a prisoner, and ahead lay a bigger unknown than the location of Cochise's rumored hoard of gold.

There was tension among the men now, and Ted knew that this was only the beginning. He was glad he was alive so he could see how it all turned out.

Red sky at night, ran silently in his mind, *sailor's delight. Red sky at morning, sailor take warning.*

"What are you smirking about?" Cavins asked when he looked at O'Hara.

"Oh, nothing. I was just thinking."

"Well, don't think, soldier boy. It might get you dead."

"If you say so," O'Hara said amiably, knowing that it was Cavins who was worried about death, not he.

🌿 Chapter 19

They rode through the night and into the dawn, Zak, Carmen, and Jimmy Chama. Zak felt the weariness in his shoulders, but there was a tingling in his toes, too, as if they were not getting enough circulation. He knew they had to stop and walk around, flex all their muscles, if they were to continue on to Tucson. It was just barely light enough to see in those moments before dawn. The world was a gray-black mass that had no definition, but still, he had seen something that gave him pause.

Carmen was sagging in her saddle, dozing or deep in sleep, he didn't know which. Chama kept rubbing his eyes, and every so often his head would droop to his chest and he'd snap it back up again as if to keep from descending into that deep sea of sleep that kept tugging at him with alluring fingers.

The day before, the two had been locked in conversation, speaking Spanish to one another, their voices barely audible to Zak. He supposed it helped them pass the time and made nothing of it. Carmen was their prisoner, but she behaved well, and perhaps he had Chama to thank for that. He heard her mention her husband's name a time or two, and Chama had spoken his name more than once as well. He figured Carmen missed her husband and welcomed having someone talk to her in her native tongue.

Moments later the dark sky of night paled, then turned bloodred as the rising sun glazed the clouds gathered on the eastern horizon. Light flooded the land with a breathtaking suddenness. Zak stared at the sanguine sunrise for a long moment, caught up in its majesty. He twisted his head and craned his neck to take it all in. A vagrant thought crossed his mind that it was like being a witness to creation itself, watching that first dawn billions of years in the past. Then he turned back to face the west and his gaze scanned the ground, picking up those hoofprints that ranged in the center of the road, bisecting the twin wagon ruts, dusted over by wind and glistening with a faint, ephemeral dew.

The first thing he noticed were the hoofprints. He'd filed them away in his mind a few days ago and had expected to see them, but was surprised at their appearance. They were fresher than they should have been. The edges should have crumbled and been more blurred. No, these were only a couple of hours old, at first glance. He reined in his horse and stepped down out of the saddle to examine them more closely.

Chama halted his horse and leaned out to see what Zak was doing. Carmen also watched, as a little shiver coursed up her spine, a gift of the chill that rose up from the earth.

"Something the matter?" Chama said.

"These tracks. Belong to a horse I watched ride

off from one of the line shacks. A horse ridden by a man named Grubb."

"Slow horse?"

"Maybe. It was kicking up dirt when Grubb rode off."

"Meaning?"

"Meaning he should have been in Tucson a day or so ago."

Zak stood up. He looked at the dawn sky, the clouds beginning to redden as if splashed by barn paint.

"Light down, you two," he said. He had seen Carmen shiver. "We all need to stretch our legs."

"I am cold," Carmen said.

"You will warm up once you get out of the saddle," Zak said. He looked down at the hoof-prints again, measuring them against the age of the wagon tracks. They each told a story, and he could gauge the passage of time. Thoughts flooded his mind. Why had Grubb delayed his journey to Tucson? Had he been following them, watching them from a distance? Why?

Whatever the answers were, Zak felt sure that Grubb would tell Ferguson and Trask that he was coming. He might even know that he had Carmen and Chama with him now. It was likely.

Chama walked around, leading his horse, flex-ing his legs. Carmen stood there, stamping first one foot, then the other, restoring circulation to her feet. She shook with the chill and flapped her arms against her body like some rain-drenched bird. The coolness rose from the ground as the sky raged in the east, a crimson tapestry so bright it seemed as if that part of the world was drenched in a fiery blood.

Zak stood up and faced the west, peering down the old road. Ahead he could see the place where it converged with the regular stage road between Tucson and Fort Bowie. He walked toward the intersection, leaving Nox standing there, reins trailing.

"I'll be back, boy," he said softly, and he caught a sharp look from Chama, who quickly looked away. Zak thought it was an odd look, and he wondered why Chama tried to conceal it. But he shook off the thought as he walked toward the convergence of the two roads.

All of the tracks led there, and he noticed that Grubb's horse had struck a different gait a few yards down the stage road. Clearly, Grubb had put the horse into a gallop, suddenly in an all-fired hurry, Zak thought.

He glanced briefly back to where Chama and Carmen were waiting. He heard Chama's voice as he spoke to her. She replied and Zak realized that they were speaking in Spanish. He caught only a word or two, but they made his skin prickle slightly. He heard *amigo,* followed quickly by its opposite, *enemigo*, then he heard Chama say, *"el gringo* Cody," which surprised him. They were talking about him, he realized, and the knowledge was disturbing. Why were they talking about him? And behind his back? He decided to wait before returning to his horse. The two had their backs turned to him, then he saw Chama step close to Carmen. He glanced over his shoulder back at Cody, then passed some-

thing to Carmen, something Zak could not see. He
saw Carmen's arms move as she tucked whatever
it was into the sash she wore around her waist. At
least that was the way he saw it. Then Chama and
Carmen turned and he could see their faces in pro-
file. Carmen glanced his way, then averted her eyes
quickly as she said something to Chama.

Her voice carried and Zak clearly heard a single
question word float from her lips.

"*Cuando?*" she said.

And Zak translated instantly. *When?*

He did not hear Chama's reply, which was only
a whisper, but he tried to fathom what Chama said
by studying his lips. As near as he could figure,
Chama had said, "*Espera.*"

"Wait."

Wait for what? Zak wondered. What had Chama
given Carmen, who was their prisoner?

Zak knew they were not far from Tucson. Another
two hours ride, maybe less. But he was on his guard
now. Something was going on between Chama and
Carmen. And it was very puzzling at that early hour.
He started walking back to his horse, and the two of
them separated. Carmen walked around, stretching
out first one leg, then the other. Chama ran a finger
under his cinch, grabbed his saddle horn and rocked
it to see if it was still on tight.

"What do you see down there?" Chama asked.

"Just where the two roads join up into a single
road. Where the stage runs to the fort."

"Yes," Chama said.

"You and Carmen had words?"

"I spoke to her. She misses her husband. She is
afraid."

"She will see him soon enough. Tucson's not far now."

"What will you do when you get there?"

Carmen turned and drifted closer to the two men. The sky was bloodred, sprawling over the entire eastern horizon like a burgundy banner, the red deepening to a crimson stain.

"See Ferguson. Call him to account. See if Lieutenant O'Hara is a prisoner there."

"You might be walking into something bad. Something dangerous."

"If so, I've walked that way before, Chama."

"Yes. I am certain that you have."

"You don't have to be with me."

"I, too, wish to find the lieutenant."

Zak knew Chama was lying. He spoke, but his words were empty, without conviction. Odd, he thought. Why would Chama lie about such a thing? And why now?"

"You don't know O'Hara, do you, Jimmy?"

"No, I don't know him."

"Why should you care what happens to him?"

Chama shrugged, as if to get Zak off the subject of Ted O'Hara.

"I guess I don't know you, either, Chama," Zak said. He would push Chama a little, see what he had in his craw.

"How can one man really know another?"

"Sometimes a man has to make quick judgments," Zak said.

"And how do you judge me, Zak?"

"I don't even have to think about that one. You come out of nowhere, with a story about being a half-breed, and I can either accept that at face value or carry a big suspicion around with me."

"And do you carry a big suspicion with you?"

Carmen walked over to the two men, stood some distance away from them. Zak noticed a slight bulge under the sash she wore around her waist. He couldn't tell from its outline what it was, but it looked a lot like a small pistol, a Derringer maybe, or a Lady Colt, or one of those small pistols Smith & Wesson made for women.

"I didn't," Zak said, "until you started lying about O'Hara."

"Lying?"

"It looks that way to me. I don't think you give a damn about O'Hara, and I think if you did run into him, you'd probably shoot him dead on the spot."

"What makes you think that?"

"A dog has reasons for running after something. I think you ran after me for a reason and it has nothing to do with the lieutenant or the Chirica-hua."

"A man can't fight suspicion. It's like a shadow when the sun is shining. It moves, but it will not go away."

"Maybe you'd better make your intentions plain, Chama, before we go any farther down the road."

Chama stiffened as if slapped. The skin on his face tautened and a hard look came into his eyes, like a shadow drifting across the sun.

"This is as far as you go, Cody," Chama said. He cocked his right hand so it hovered just over the butt of his pistol. Zak saw Carmen jerk straight and her right hand brush against the top of her sash.

Zak looked at the two without making a move himself. Seconds ticked by, and it was so quiet, it seemed all three were holding their breaths at the same time.

"Maybe you'd better think about that for a minute, Chama," Zak said evenly. "Words like you just said can shorten a man's life real quick."

"I have thought about it, Cody. End of the line for you. Sorry."

"Any reason?"

Carmen spoke, to both men's surprise.

"You killed his brother, Cody, you bastard."

"That so?" Zak said, looking straight at Chama. "It's news to me."

"Felipe Lopez," Chama said.

"He was your brother?"

"My half brother. We had the same mother. I loved him."

"Like you, Chama, Felipe had a choice. To live or die."

"I do not know how you did it. I know I found him dead, and your tracks."

"So, you tracked me, and waited. Why now?"

"Because you will not get to Tucson alive. There is too much at stake. I want Hiram to win this one. The Apaches are our enemy."

"You are not Apache," Zak said.

Chama spat, his features crinkled in disgust.

"Filth," he said.

"You have the Indian blood."

"Not Apache. They killed my parents, held me and Felipe prisoner until we both became men and got away from them. I have the Comanche blood."

Suddenly it all became clear. Zak understood. He had allowed himself to be duped. He had believed Chama's story. But there had been no reason to doubt it. He took a man at his word until he proved out as a liar. Now Chama had proven out.

"I guess you got cause to hate, Chama," Zak said.

"You are in the way, Cody, and you killed my brother. Now you will die."

Zak looked at Carmen, then back to Chama.

"Two against one, I reckon."

"Yes," Chama said, and gone was the sleepiness, the fatigue. Carmen had brightened up, too, was licking her lips like a hungry cat.

These two meant to kill him, for sure, gun him down like a dog and leave him for wolf meat.

Still, Zak did not move. He knew he did not have to, just yet.

The hand had been dealt. And, in death, as in life, the hand had to be played out.

He was ready.

Fate would decide who had the better hand.

Zak knew that when it came to a showdown, most men often made a fatal mistake in that moment just before a gun was drawn or a trigger pulled.

And that gave him the advantage. Always.

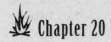 **Chapter 20**

The eastern sky drained its blood, turned to ashes. Tiny mares' tails began to etch the sky with Arabic scrawls of stormy portent. Zak did not look up at the wisps, but kept his gaze fastened on Chama and Carmen. A slight breeze began to rise, its fingers tousling Carmen's hair as she stood there, her face a mask of defiance and determination.

"Tell me, Chama," Zak said, "did you have anything to do with Lieutenant O'Hara's capture? You carry yourself like a military man."

"I was there, yes. I told Ben where the patrol would be and when the best time would be to take O'Hara prisoner."

"You're a deserter, then," Zak said.

Chama shrugged. "I have done my time in the army. I was a sergeant. A good place for a spy like me, do you not think? That is finished. I go now to fight the Apache, to help Hiram and Ben wipe them out. To take their gold."

Zak caught the boastful tone in Chama's voice. Let him brag, he thought.

"The Chiricahua have no gold."

"Cochise has gold. Much gold."

Zak suppressed a laugh. This was far too serious for humor.

"That is an old wives' tale. A lie," Zak said. "Rather, it is a lie made by white men to turn the settlers against Cochise. He has no gold, beyond a few trinkets."

"That is not what Trask and Ferguson believe. And I think O'Hara knows where that gold is. He will tell us. We will find it."

"Not a good reason to die, Chama. For a pile of gold that is only a fairy tale told by white men."

"As I told you, Cody, this is as far as you go. We are two against one, Carmen and I. You can drop your gun now and I will let you walk away. We will keep your horse."

"My horse is worth more than any Apache gold," Zak said softly.

"He is not worth your life, Cody."

"Chama, let me ask you something before you draw your pistol."

"Ask," Chama said, flexing the fingers of his gun hand. "You do not have much time, gringo."

It was funny, Zak thought, how quickly people could change, how swiftly they could change their colors, like a chameleon. Chama had all these pent-up emotions inside of him that he had been carrying for many miles. Now, in the light of a new day, he had reverted to what he always was, a lying, scheming, shifty sonofabitch with murder on his mind.

"Ever stand on a high cliff and look down, wonder what it would be like to fall about a hundred feet onto the rocks below?" Zak asked.

"No, I never have done that. You ask a strange question. Why? Do you have the fear of falling, Cody?"

"No. I was just thinking to myself about you. And me."

"There is nothing to think about," Chama said.

"Chama, I'm that tall cliff, and you're standing right on the edge of it, about to fall right off. Only in your case, you're never going to see the ground before you hit it."

The expression on Chama's face changed as he realized what Zak had said. In that moment, he knew that Zak had turned the tables on him. Zak was calling him out, not the other way around.

"All right," Chama said, and went into a crouch. As he did, his right hand stabbed downward for the butt of his pistol.

Zak was facing the sunrise, but he did not look at it. Instead, he kept his gaze focused on Chama, and in the periphery of his vision, on Carmen. He was aware of Chama's intentions with the first twitch of his hand, which echoed on his face like a tic.

Zak stood straight, his gaze locked on Chama's flickering eyes. But in one smooth motion his hand snaked down to his pistol, drew it from its holster as if it was oiled, his thumb cocking it before it cleared leather.

Carmen was slow to react, but she saw Chama grab for his pistol and she became galvanized into action. Her hand slid inside her sash, grasped the butt of the pistol Chama had given her and began to slide it upward. She appeared to be moving fast, but in that warped time frame when death dangles by a slender hair, her motion was much too slow, like an inching snail trying to escape a juggernaut.

Zak's Walker Colt roared just as Chama's barrel cleared the holster. He shot from just below his hip, the barrel at a thirty-degree angle. Just enough, Zak thought, to put Chama down.

Chama opened his mouth and yelled, "Noooooo," as Zak's pistol barked. The bullet caught him just above the belt buckle, driving into him like a twenty-pound maul, smashing through flesh as it mushroomed on its way out his back, nearly doubling the size of its soft lead point.

The air rushed out of Chama's lungs like the gush from a blacksmith's bellows and he staggered backward, blood gushing from his abdomen, a crimson fountain. He groaned and went to his knees, the pistol still clutched in his hand. He tried to raise it for a shot at Zak, then his eyes went wide as Zak took careful aim and blasted off another shot that took away Chama's scream as it ripped through his mouth and blew away three inches of his spine in a paralyzing crunch of bone.

Carmen slid her pistol from the sash and pointed it at Zak, her hand trembling, her arm swaying as she tried to aim.

"Sorry, Carmen," Zak said, "but you're standing on the edge of that same cliff."

She fired and the bullet whistled past Zak's ear. He stood there, shook his head slightly and pulled the trigger of his Colt. Carmen closed her eyes for a moment, then opened them in disbelief as the bullet spun her halfway around. Blood spurted from her shoulder, but she managed to lift her pistol again and aim it at Zak, her lips pressed together in rage and defiance. She looked like a cornered animal, her brown eyes flickering with flinty sparks. The pistol cracked and the bullet plowed a furrow in the ground between Zak's legs. He still stood straight, and now his eyes narrowed as he cocked the pistol and held it at arm's length in a straight line that pointed directly at her heart.

"Sorry, Carmen," he said as he squeezed the trigger. "But you called the tune."

The bullet smashed into Carmen's chest, slightly to the left of her breastbone. Her heart exploded under the impact as the bullet flattened and expanded after smashing through ribs. She dropped like a sash weight, a crimson stain blossoming on her chest. She lay like a broken flower in the dirt, the angry expression wiped from her face as if someone had swiped it with a towel. Her eyes glazed over with the frost of death, staring sightlessly at the sky.

The sound of the last gunshot faded into a deathly silence as Zak ejected the hulls from his pistol and slid fresh cartridges into the empty chambers. The smell of burnt gunpowder lingered in his nostrils as he gazed down at Carmen's body, shaking his head at another needless and useless death. Whatever scraps life had offered her, he had taken them all away, regretfully.

Zak saw that Chama, too, was stone dead, his bleeding stopped. He had tried to warn him, but Chama's self-confidence bordered on insane arrogance. The man had followed his own path to the end of the road. The road ended on a high cliff and Chama had taken the fall. The stench from his body, since he had voided himself, was strong, and Zak turned away.

Death was such an ugly thing, he thought. One moment a man, or a woman, was vibrant with energy, brimming with life. The next, after death, they were just carrion, all signs of life and personality gone, their bodies like cast-off rattlesnake skins. In Tibet, he knew, when a person died, the monks took his body to a place in the hills where there was a convex slab of rock. The dead body was stripped and men cut it into pieces, tossed the parts to the large waiting vultures. Their idea was to remove all traces of humanness and let the soul return to spirit form. They watched the vultures gorge themselves on human remains, then take to the sky, flying over the hills and the mountains, carrying what was left of the human corpse. The sight gave the mourners great comfort.

Zak sighed and turned away to walk toward his horse.

Nox stood there in silence, his ears still flattened, his body braced for danger.

Then the horse's ears pricked up and twisted as if to catch a distant sound.

Zak paid attention to such things. He stopped and listened, turning his head first one way, then the other. The sun was clearing the horizon, sliding up through murky logjams of clouds, spraying the land with a pale gold in its broad reach.

He heard the familiar click of a rifle cocking, and whirled to see an armed soldier pointing a Spencer repeating rifle straight at him.

"You just hold on there," the soldier said.

A moment later Zak heard the scuffle of a horse's hooves and turned his head to see another soldier, also armed with a Spencer, bearing down on him from behind a low hill.

"Better lift them hands, mister," the first soldier said.

Zak slowly lifted his hands.

"Looks to me like we got a murder here," the second soldier said, then turned and raised a hand, beckoning to someone Zak could not see.

The two soldiers closed in on Zak, flanking him on both sides, but kept their distance, their barrels trained on him, their fingers caressing the triggers.

The Spencer had a seven-cartridge magazine, tubular, and used .56/56 rimfire cartridges. Zak knew they could shoot him to pieces at such close range.

"This wasn't murder, soldier," Zak said softly. "Self-defense."

"So you say."

"Look at the bodies. They both have pistols next to them."

"You just hold steady there."

Then Colleen O'Hara rode up. She stared at the bodies of Chama and Carmen, gasped aloud. Then she saw Zak. She stopped her horse next to the second soldier.

"Mr. Cody," she said. "Whatever happened here? Did you kill that man and that woman?"

"You know this jasper?" the first soldier asked.

"Why, yes. Slightly. Why are you pointing your guns at him?"

"It appears that Mr. Cody murdered these two people and I'm going to take him into custody."

"Mr. Scofield, Delbert, I think you may be making

a big mistake," Colleen said. "I'm sure Mr. Cody has some reasonable explanation."

"Yeah, what is your explanation, Cody?" the second soldier said.

"Your name?" Cody said, looking at the soldier.

"This is Hugo," Colleen said, "Hugo Rivers. These two were escorting me to Tucson where I plan to look for my brother Ted."

"Well, Private Rivers," Zak said, "these two pulled pistols on me and were going to kill me. I beat them to the punch."

"Some story," Rivers said.

Scofield snorted. Then, he looked at Chama more closely.

"Hey, this here's Sergeant Jimmy Chama," Scofield explained. "He's a damned deserter."

River turned his head to look at Chama. "Sure as hell looks like him," he said.

"That is Chama," Zak said. "Miss O'Hara, he's the one who fixed things with Ferguson and Trask so they could kidnap your brother."

Colleen reared back in her saddle, her back stiffening.

"He is?" she said.

"That's what he told me," Zak said. "He was proud of it. He is a deserter, as these men say. Or was."

"What about that woman?" Scofield asked. "She wasn't no deserter."

"She's married to one of Ferguson's men. She was my prisoner. Chama slipped her a pistol and they both meant to kill me, to stop me from trying to free Lieutenant O'Hara."

"Well, we'll just have to sort all this out," Scofield said.

"No," Zak said, dropping his hands, "you two are now under my command. Put down those rifles. We've got a ways to ride."

"You ain't got no authority to order us to do a damned thing, mister," Rivers said.

"I think he does," Colleen said. "I learned, at the fort, that Mr. Cody is a commissioned officer in the army, working for General Crook and President Grant. You're a colonel, are you not, Mr. Cody?"

Zak nodded.

The two soldiers looked at him, their faces dumbstruck.

Before they could say anything, Colleen lifted her head and pointed to the west.

"I see a cloud of dust," she said. "Somebody's coming this way. Or, it might be the stage."

Zak walked quickly to Nox and climbed into the saddle.

"All of you," he said, "follow me to cover behind that hill over there. Until we know who that is under that dust cloud, we're all in danger."

Colleen was the first to move. Reluctantly, the two soldiers followed.

"There goes our damned leave," Rivers grumbled.

"You trust this Cody?"

"He's the onliest one who seems to know what the hell he's doin', I reckon."

Scofield stifled a curse.

The dust cloud grew closer as the four riders galloped behind the low hill well off the old wagon road.

The sun filled the sky and the blue heavens filled with mares' tails as if the gods had gone mad and scrawled their warning of impending weather for all to see.

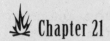 **Chapter 21**

Trask pulled his hat brim down to shield his eyes from the rising sun. But as he gazed at the sky ahead, he saw the first buzzard float to a point and begin circling. The bird was soon joined by two more, then, as they rode on toward the junction of the two wagon roads, several more gathered and began to circle.

"What do you make of it, Hiram?" Ben asked. "Too many buzzards for a dead jackrabbit."

"It don't look natural," Ferguson said. "Must be a big chunk of dead meat to draw that many turkeys this early of a morning."

"That's what I'm thinkin'," Trask said.

He turned in the saddle and looked at the men riding behind until he picked the face of the man he wanted.

"Deets, come on up here," Trask yelled, beckoning with his hand.

Deets rode up alongside Trask.

"Al, see them buzzards up yonder?" Trask said.

"Hell, you can't miss 'em. That's all we been lookin' at for the past five minutes."

"You ride on up under 'em and see what it is they're sniffin'."

"A dead cow, maybe."

"You check, Al. Be quick about it. You get in trouble, you fire off a shot. Got it?"

"Sure, boss," Deets said, and slapped his horse's rump with his reins. He galloped off and the men in line began talking among themselves.

Trask turned around again. "Shut up," he said, and the men fell silent.

Ferguson suppressed the urge to snort at Trask's remark. He didn't want to rile the man up any more than he already was. Trask had been in a foul mood all morning, snapping at the men, cursing the sunrise, the flies, the chill that rose from the earth earlier. He had a lot in his craw and the sight of the buzzards wasn't doing his mood any damned good.

Trask watched Deets disappear over a rise. The buzzards dipped lower, circling like slow-motion leaves caught in a slow-motion whirlwind. More buzzards had flown in to take their places on the invisible carousel, and Trask unconsciously sniffed the air for the stench of death.

Deets was taking a long time, it seemed, but when Trask looked up at the sky again, he saw that the vultures were at least a quarter mile from him, maybe more. Still, he didn't like to wait, and he put spurs to his horse's flanks. The men behind him did the same. Ferguson frowned. They had a long ride ahead of them, days of it, and Trask was already wearing out their horses.

Ted O'Hara saw the buzzards, too, and knew that the sight of them had agitated Trask. This gave him a twinge of pleasure. Trask was a man who had to be in control at all times, he surmised. When he felt that control slipping, he turned ugly and mean. The gallop wouldn't accomplish much over the stretch of land they had yet to cover, but he knew Trask had sent Deets up ahead to investigate, and yet, didn't fully trust any of his men. In fact, he probably trusted no man, and that was almost always a fatal flaw. The loner could only go so far in life. Then, when he began to run out of friends, he stood completely alone, and without anyone to rely on, except himself, he was lost. Trask wasn't at that point yet, but he was certainly headed for it. One of his men, one day, would become fed up with him and put a bullet in his back. And Trask would never know what hit him. He brooked no counsel, took no advice. From anyone, except himself.

The line of men stretched out into a ragged column as the slower riders fell behind, but nobody complained. All of them knew where Trask was headed, just under those circling buzzards, and all would eventually reach it. Some of the men exchanged knowing looks, but kept their comments to themselves.

Trask topped the rise and slowed his horse.

There was Deets, riding back and forth across the old road. He was leaning over, scanning the ground. He rode toward the regular stage road where it had veered off from the old road, then back again, beyond where two saddled horses stood and there were two dark objects on the ground that Trask could not identify as being human or animal.

The men behind him caught up and fanned out

to look at what Trask was seeing. None spoke a word, at first. They all just stared at Deets, trying to figure out what he was doing.

As if reading their thoughts, Trask said, "Studying tracks."

Julio Delgado broke the silence among the men following Trask.

"That is the horse of my wife down there," he said. "The brown one with the blaze face."

"I know the other one," Hector Gonzalez said. "Do you not recognize it, Fidel?"

"Yes, I know that horse, too," Hector's brother said.

The Mexicans all grew very excited. They slapped each other on the arms and exchanged knowing looks.

"That is the horse of Jimmy Chama," Renaldo Valdez said. "*Ay de mi.*"

"Chama, ain't he the boy what set up O'Hara for the capture?" Trask asked.

"Yep, he's the one. A sergeant in the army out at the fort. But he said he was going to desert as soon as my men got away clean with O'Hara."

"What's his horse doing there, I wonder," Grissom said. "And him not on it."

"Carmen, oh Carmencita," Julio breathed, "'onde stas?"

He twisted the reins in his hands as if he wanted to strangle someone.

"Let's go see what we got," Trask said, and dug spurs into his horse's flanks.

Deets rode off toward a long low hill on his left. He stopped his horse, then looked at all of the other hills, a jumble of them, rising on either side and behind. He turned his horse and rode back to where the other horses stood and where the dead bodies lay. He kept looking back over his shoulder and then he rubbed a spot behind his neck.

As he rode closer, Trask saw that the dark shapes on the ground were human. And they were dead. A man and a woman.

"Al," he said as Deets rode up.

"Found 'em like this," Deets said. "That's what brung them buzzards."

"What do you make of it?" Trask asked, looking down at the body of Chama.

"Still tryin' to sort it all out, Ben. Near as I can figger, they was three riders—Chama, that lady yonder, and one other. He might have kilt them two lyin' on the ground, or some other riders come up and they could have kilt 'em, but that don't make no sense, maybe."

"What do you mean?"

"Three riders come from over yonder like they was ridin' the stage road to Tucson. Then the tracks show four of them rode off toward them hills yonder." Deets pointed in the direction from which he had just come.

"So, we're dealing with four riders," Trask said.

"Looks thataway. Less'n there's more about."

"What the hell do you mean, Al?"

"I mean, these are the onliest tracks I seen, Ben. Maybe this was some kind of bushwhack, and four people jumped these two, then rejoined their outfit. Could be the army, I reckon."

"Shit," Trask said.

The others crowded around to listen to what Deets had to say. Julio Delgado rode over to the

body of his wife and dismounted. He bent over
her and began to sob. Renaldo looked over at him
and then rode his horse up close and dismounted.
He patted Julio on the back. Then he, too, began
to weep, so quietly the others could not hear. The
other Mexicans drifted over, one by one, to con-
sole the grief-stricken Julio, who was cradling his
dead wife in his arms and rocking slowly back and
forth.

O'Hara suppressed a smile. This was not a military operation, but Trask was too dumb to see it.

Ferguson looked at Chama's face, then turned
away, as if death were too much for him in the
harsh light of day. He gulped in fresh air to keep
from gagging on the smell.

Trask looked over at O'Hara. "You know that
man there?" he asked.

"He was a sergeant," O'Hara said. "Rode with
our patrol."

"You know anything about this?"

"Not any more than you do, Trask. Two people
dead. Probably killed by gunshots."

"You're not as smart as you might think you are,
O'Hara."

O'Hara said nothing. He kept his face blank, impassive as desert stone.

Trask turned back to Deets. "The tracks lead
over yonder, right?"

"Right, boss. I figure they circled that long hill
and either lit a shuck or are watching us right
now."

Trask scanned the top of the ridge. Everything
looked the same. Rocks, cactus, dirt. He saw nothing move, saw no sign of life anywhere.

"Well, if there was an army waiting up there, they could have picked us off by now. We're riding on."

"Aren't we going to bury these two?" Ferguson asked.

"I don't give a damn," Trask said. "We've already wasted enough time here." He looked up at the sky. "Them buzzards got to eat, too."

"I will bury my wife," Julio said. "And Chama, too." He crossed himself.

Trask fixed him with a look of contempt. "Do whatever you want, Delgado. We're ridin' on. You'd better catch up."

"I will catch up," Julio said, biting hard to cut back on his anger.

"I will help Julio," Renaldo said. "It will not take too long."

"I, too, will stay and help dig the graves," Manuel Diego said.

Trask headed straight up the old road, Deets, Ferguson, Cavins, and O'Hara right behind him. The others trailed after them as Julio and Renaldo drew their knives and began cutting into the hard pan of the desert. Julio's face was streaked with grimy tears and he was shaking as he dug.

"That bastard Trask," he said, in English. *"Un hijo de puta, salvaje."*

"Calm yourself, Julio," Renaldo said in Spanish. "One day, perhaps, we will bury him."

"That would give me much satisfaction," Julio said.

He picked up the small pistol lying next to his wife, examined it and stuck it under his belt.

"I wonder where she got this pistol," he said softly.

Renaldo shrugged.

Trask turned to Ferguson when they had traveled a short distance.

"I know who killed that Chama and Carmen Delgado," he said.

"You do? How? Who?"

"Cody," Trask said. "He's in this, somewhere."

"How do you know?" Ferguson asked.

"I just know. I know it in my gut, that sonofabitch. I figure Chama made a mistake, or maybe went for his gun. The woman, she may have thrown down on Cody, too. That bastard's fast. Very fast. He sure as hell could have killed them both. And I know damned well he did."

"Who are the other riders, then?"

"I don't know. I wish I did, but I just don't know, damn it all."

He rolled a quirly and stuck it in his mouth. He lit a match and drew the smoke in. Ferguson got very quiet, but kept looking off to his left at the jumble of hills and the long ridge that seemed to be the land brooding down on them.

Over on the ridge there was just the slightest movement as Cody peered down at the old road.

He moved so slowly and held his head so still, he might have been just another rock to anyone glancing up at him. He was hatless, and his face, browned from the sun, was not much different in color than the desert itself.

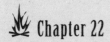 **Chapter 22**

Zak clamped a hand over Colleen's mouth and pushed her down, held her hard against the rocky ground. Her eyes flashed with a wild look as she struggled against him. The two soldiers looked on, uncertain about what they should do.

"Listen, Miss O'Hara," Zak said, his voice a throaty whisper, "you make one sound and we'll be captured and killed. Do you understand me?"

She calmed down, but Zak kept up the pressure on her mouth and body.

"I mean it. Those are dangerous men down there and they outnumber us."

She tried to nod her head. Her eyes flashed her response.

"You'll behave, then?" he asked.

"Umm-ummm," she replied.

"I'll let up on you," he whispered, "but if you cry out or make noise, I'll knock you cold. If you have anything to say, you whisper right into my ear as the sound won't travel. Got it?"

"Mmmm-hmmm."

Zak slowly lifted his hand from her mouth, but kept it hovering a couple of inches away. He

watched her lips like a man watching a burning
fuse on a stick of dynamite. He nodded and backed
away so she could sit up. She beckoned to him,
asking him to come close.

She put her lips right up against his ear.

"That's Ted down there. My brother," she hissed
in a sizzling whisper.

"Nothing we can do about it now. But we'll get
him free. I promise. Now, just keep that notion in
your head and shut up."

She nodded.

Zak signed with his hands to the two soldiers,
telling them he was going to crawl to the top of the
ridge and that they were to stay there, out of sight,
with Colleen. Both men nodded assent.

Before Zak crept to the top of the ridge, Colleen
drew him close and whispered softly in his ear.
She put one hand behind his head and pulled him
next to her so his arm brushed against one of her
breasts.

"I wish," she sighed softly, "you were still holding me down, Zak."

Zak felt the strength drain from his knees and his
stomach fluttered with a thousand flying insects.
The musky scent of her assailed his nostrils like
coal oil thrown on an open flame. His veins sizzled
with excitement and there was a twinge at his loins
as the fever of her touch and the urgency of her
words seared through him like wildfire.

He drew away from her, slowly, and touched a
finger to his lips. She smiled at him, and he felt
his insides melt as if she had poured molten honey
down his throat. He turned from her and began
the slow crawl to a vantage point on the ridgetop

where he could watch and listen. He mentally shook off what had happened, needing to focus, to concentrate.

He lay very still, his head resting on his hands between two head-sized rocks. He saw Trask, the man he took to be Ferguson, and the Mexicans congregating around the body of Carmen Delgado. And he saw Ted O'Hara, guarded by one man in particular. O'Hara looked at ease, however, and Zak mentally applauded his courage, his coolness. He saw a man who was more alert than any of the others, a prisoner who refused to allow his chains to weigh him down. Ted O'Hara, he decided, was a good man to ride the river with.

He saw Trask extend his arm toward the east and start to ride up the old road, the others following in his wake. The Mexicans continued to dig a grave for Carmen as Trask and the others moved out of eyesight.

Zak thought for a moment. It was pretty plain where Trask was headed. He had left the stage road and was traveling on the old road, straight into the heart of Apache lands. There was only one thing Ben Trask was interested in, Zak knew—gold. Apache gold. And if his hunch was right, he was using O'Hara to lead him straight to an Apache camp. O'Hara had been dealing with the Apaches and he knew where their strongholds were. Like Jeffords, he most likely had spoken with Cochise and probably knew more than any other man in the territory.

O'Hara was in a bad spot.

And so were they all, for that matter.

Zak didn't wait for the Mexicans to finish digging the grave for Carmen. Three of them stayed behind, and he knew it would take them some time to finish digging with their knives. If they buried Chama, it would take longer. The longer the better, he thought. But he knew he would have to deal with them sooner or later.

He slowly slid back off the ridgetop and descended to where Colleen and the two soldiers were still waiting. Colleen's face told him that she was anxious, while the two soldiers seemed restless and ill at ease, perhaps put out because they had been left with nothing to do.

"Have they all gone?" Colleen asked in a whisper.

"Most of them," Zak said softly. He knew his voice wouldn't carry over the hill to the other side.

"How many?" asked Scofield.

"More than you two could handle. It's not safe to leave yet. Some Mexicans are burying the dead woman. But I reckon you all are anxious to get to Tucson."

"Yes, sir," Rivers said. "I mean, we have leave, Delbert and me."

"Well, I'm certainly not going to Tucson," Colleen said, her voice pitched low. "Not while those rascals have my brother. If I have to, I'll chase them to the ends of the earth."

Zak gave her a sharp look. "I think you ought to go to Tucson, Miss O'Hara. Under the escort of Scofield and Rivers. It would be the safest thing to do."

"No. I came this far to find my brother. Well, I've found him and I'm going to . . ."

"To what?" Zak asked.

"Well, I have a gun. A pistol. I can shoot. I'm going to get Ted away from those despicable people."

"Ben Trask would shoot you dead in your tracks if you even came after him with a pair of scissors, let alone a pistol."

Colleen huffed in indignation.

Scofield stepped forward. "What you aim to do, Colonel? You can't go after all them men by yourself."

"That's my field problem," Zak said.

"It don't need to be."

"You have no stake in this. You and Rivers are on leave."

"You got any plan at all, Colonel Cody?"

Zak looked at the two men, measuring their willingness to give up their leave and help him fight a force that outnumbered them.

Buzzards floated in the sky like leaves drifting on the wind.

"Once Trask and his bunch get far enough away, I'll brace those three Mexicans," Zak said. "The sound of gunfire will draw Trask right back down on me if I shoot now."

"You're going to kill those poor Mexicans?" Colleen whispered, without any sign of enmity in her voice.

"I'll make them an offer," Zak said.

"An offer?"

"They can walk away. Go back to town."

"And will they?"

Zak cocked his head and looked at her as he would an addled child.

"One of those men is burying his wife, the woman I killed. He'll want blood for blood."

Colleen shivered. "It seems such a shame," she said. "All the killing."

"That's why you ought to go with these boys on into Tucson."

"I'm not going anywhere without my brother. Now I know where he is, I'll not give up."

"We feel the same way," Scofield said. "Lieutenant O'Hara's a mighty fine soldier."

"That's right," Rivers said. "'Sides, you can't go up against three men all by yourself. Me 'n' Delbert can even up the odds."

"Then you'll take Miss O'Hara into Tucson?" Zak said.

"I'm not going to Tucson," she hissed, her whisper loud as bacon sizzling in a fry pan.

"I'll be tracking near a dozen men, Miss O'Hara. Any one of which would shoot you dead without a second thought."

"You don't think I'd shoot back?"

"You might. But would you shoot first, before any one of them got the drop on you, Miss O'Hara?"

"Yes," she said, her voice firm and filled with conviction. "Yes, I would. My father and my brother didn't just teach me how to shoot. They taught me how to defend myself. And stop calling me Miss O'Hara like I'm some frail waif who needs coddling. And I'll call you Zak, if you don't mind."

"I think you've been out in the hot sun too long, Colleen," Zak said.

She gave a low "humph" and glared at him.

"All right," Zak said, looking at the two soldiers. "You want to mix in, I could use your help."

"We do," Scofield said. "What's your plan?"

Cody was ticking off minutes in his mind, minutes and distance, figuring Trask was keeping up a steady pace to the east. Soon, he thought, he would be out of earshot of any gunfire. Maybe. Sound carried far in the clear dry desert air.

"Rivers," Zak said, "how good are you with that Fogarty carbine?"

Rivers looked down at the rifle in his hand.

"This is a Spencer rifle," he said. "Army issue."

"Spencer sold his company to a man named Fogarty. Can you shoot it true?"

"Yes, sir, Colonel, sir. I'm the best shot in the outfit."

"He is," Scofield said. "And I'm right next to him."

"Colleen, I don't want you in this. You stay here. Scofield, you climb that ridge about two hundred yards to the east. Rivers, you climb up from here. Real slow. Soon as I round the end of this hill and you don't see me, you start your climb. Stay low and move slow. I'll ride up on those boys and tell 'em 'what for,' and you should be in position by then. Any one of them goes for his gun, you open up."

"We'll do 'er," Scofield said.

Zak walked to his horse, climbed into the saddle.

Colleen came up to him, grabbed his hand, clasped it in hers.

"Zak," she said, her whispery voice like silk sliding on silk, "be careful. I want you to come back alive."

"I will, Colleen. Just sit tight. Try to think of something pleasant."

She squeezed his hand. "I'll think about you, Zak."

He turned his horse and rode off toward the lowest point of the hill. He did not look back, but he felt three pairs of eyes burning into his back.

He slipped the Colt in and out of its holster twice, then seated it loosely in its leather sheath. In the distance he heard a quail pipe its fluting call, and above him the buzzards wheeled on air currents, so close he could see their homely heads, their jeweled eyes, sharp beaks, as they moved their heads from side to side.

To the northwest he thought he saw a blackening sky, but he couldn't be sure. The day was young and the blue sky marked only with long trailing wisps of clouds that looked like smoke from a far-away fire.

Trask should be far enough away by now, he thought. He hoped the Mexicans would take his advice and ride back to Tucson without a fight.

It was a long shot, but he'd make them the offer.

But he was ready.

For anything.

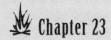 **Chapter 23**

Julio Delgado heard a sound. He looked up from the shallow grave, squinted until his eyes were in focus on the rider coming toward them from the west. Renaldo Valdez saw him and turned his head, looking off in the same direction.

"Someone is coming," Julio said.

"I see him. Who is it?"

"I do not know."

Manuel Diego set down a rock he had dug up and turned to look.

"Maybe that is the man who killed your wife, Julio," he said.

"Maybe," Delgado said, his voice low and guttural.

A few of the buzzards landed some distance from the gravesite. They flexed their wings and marched to and fro like tattered generals surveying a battlefield. Their squawks scratched the air like chalk screeching on a blackboard.

"He does not ride fast," Renaldo Valdez said. "He does not hurry."

"No," Delgado said. "He is without hurry on that black horse."

"He wears black like the horse, eh?" Diego observed. "Maybe he is a messenger."

"A messenger? Who would send a messenger out here from Tucson?" Delgado wiped tears from under his eyes, squinted again.

"Maybe there is trouble at the office of Ferguson," Diego said. "Maybe it burned down."

"You have the imagination of a chicken," Valdez said.

"Why not?" Delgado said. "He has the brains of a chicken."

Valdez laughed. Diego did not laugh.

Delgado stood up. He did not dust himself off, but continued to stare at the approaching rider. Valdez and Diego got to their feet as well, slowly, knives still gripped loosely in their hands.

"You there," Delgado called to Cody, "what brings you this way?" He spoke in English.

"I have a message for you," Cody said.

"See?" Diego said. "He has a message. *El es un mensajero.*"

"You are full of the shit, Manuel," Valdez said.

"Be quiet," Delgado said.

Zak drew closer. "What message do you bring?" Delgado asked.

"I will tell you in a minute," Zak said.

"Tell me now, mister. Do not come any closer. It is very dangerous here."

Zak kept riding.

"Oh, yes, it is dangerous here," he said. "Dangerous for you. Are you Delgado?"

"Yes, I am Julio Delgado. You have news for me?"

"If you are Julio Delgado, I do have news for you. And for your companions as well."

Zak rode up to the three men and reined in Nox. He looked down at them. Delgado's knife lay on the ground, but Valdez and Diego still clutched theirs, more tightly than before.

"And what is this news that is so important that you ride out all the way from Tucson?"

"I did not ride from Tucson," Zak said. "I rode out of the night on this black horse. My message is this: If you and your companions will bury your dead and ride back to Tucson instead of catching up to Trask and Ferguson, you will live another day. Maybe many more days."

Zak's words hung there like black bunting in a funeral parlor. Delgado cleared his throat. Valdez and Diego looked at each other.

"He is loco," Valdez said in Spanish.

"He said he rides out of the night? What does he mean?" Diego asked, also in Spanish.

"Why do you want us to go back to town?" Delgado said to Zak. "Are you going to kill us if we do not do this?"

"Yes, Delgado," Zak said. "I'm going to kill you if you try and join up with Ben Trask. I am going to kill him, too."

"Who are you?"

"I am Zak Cody."

"You are the one they call the Shadow Rider?"

"Some call me that, yes."

"I am not afraid of you, Cody. Did you kill my wife? A man told me that you did."

"I killed your wife, Delgado. And I killed Chama, too."

Delgado's neck swelled up like a bull in the rut. His face purpled with rage. The blood drained from the faces of Valdez and Diego. They both looked as if someone had come up to them and kicked them in the nuts.

"*Hijo de mala leche.*" Delgado spat. Then, in English, "You bastard."

"He is only one. We are three," Valdez said in Spanish to the others.

"He might kill one of us," Diego said.

"I will kill him," Delgado said. "For what he did."

Zak understood every word.

He slid quickly from the saddle, slapped Nox on the rump and squared off to face the three men.

"What do you wish, Delgado?" Zak said in Spanish. "To bury your wife and ride to the town alive, or leave her body to the buzzards while you join her in sleep?"

"You talk very brave, gringo."

Diego and Valdez squeezed the handles of their knives. Cody was too far away. Diego let his knife slide through his fingers until he grasped only the tip.

Zak saw the move and waited.

Delgado licked his dry lips. A buzzard squawked, impatient. There was a silence after that, a silence buried deep in a soundless well.

"You are a dead man, gringo," Delgado said in English. "You do not tell me what to do."

"Delgado, it is your choice. But I will tell you this. The last sound you hear on this earth will be the voice of my Walker Colt."

Delgado's face grew livid with rage. He went into a crouch and clawed for the butt of his pistol.

Diego started to draw his arm back to throw his knife at Cody. Valdez stabbed his hand downward to jerk his pistol free.

A single second splintered into fractions. Four lives teetered on the fulcrum of eternity. All breathing stopped. Sweat froze. Eyes crackled and sparked like tiny flames deep in men's souls. Time no longer existed in that place. Somewhere, out of sight, a small door opened just a crack and there was a darkness beyond, a limitless darkness where no light could shine.

Cody's hand was a flash of lightning, his pistol a thundercrack in the mute firmament. The blue sky seemed to pale as fire belched from the barrel of his pistol and the hornet sound of his Colt fried the still morning air. Delgado sucked blood from the hole in his throat and his arms flew upward, his hands empty.

Cody sidestepped as he hammered back and his pistol roared again. The bullet caught Diego just as he hurled his knife and before Diego hit the ground, Cody knocked the hammer back on the Colt with the heel of his left hand and swung the barrel toward Valdez, who had his pistol nearly out of its holster. His lips were pressed together as if he were under a great strain.

"*Hijo* . . ." he breathed as Cody's pistol roared with the exploding sound of doom. The bullet smashed into Valdez's chest with the force of a pile driver, cracking bone, crushing flesh and veins into raw pulp, and his eyes clouded up as tears shot from ducts like a salty rain.

Valdez collapsed to his knees and struggled to

draw breath into lungs that were clogged with blood and bone. Then the feeble light in his eyes fled through that open door, into the darkness.

Zak cocked his pistol again and looked at each man sprawled on the ground, the smoke from his pistol rising like a fakir's cobra from a wicker basket, the air reeking of burnt powder.

He heard a noise then, the clattering of rocks, the crash of brush. He turned to see Hugo Rivers running headlong down the slope of the hill, his rifle held high over his head, his feet moving almost too fast for his body to follow.

"Hey," Rivers yelled, "you done it all. I didn't have a chance to help."

Zak opened the gate on the pistol and began ejecting the brass hulls. He had filled the empty cylinders with fresh cartridges by the time Rivers reached his side, out of breath and panting. In the distance, he saw Scofield running toward them at a fast lope.

"Boy, sir, I never saw nothin' like that. I mean, one minute they was three men bracin' you, and you plumb beat 'em all to the draw and dusted them off like they was flies on a buttermilk pail."

"There is an old saying about the quick and the dead, Rivers."

"Yeah, what's that, sir?"

"If you aren't quick, you're dead."

"Never heard that."

"I just made it up. You'd better get your horses and Miss O'Hara. Don't let her see any of this, though. I'll meet you on the other end of the hill, the top end."

"Yes, sir. Right away, sir. But I'm still tryin' to figure out how you was so much faster than any of them. They wasn't slow."

"When a man goes for his gun, Rivers, he'd better not have anything else on his mind. Those men were so busy trying to figure out what to do about me, they forgot I was there."

"Well, no, sir, they knew you was there all right. That one boy, the one you shot first, well, he went for his gun long before you did."

"He might have gone for it, Rivers, but I was already there, about two seconds ahead of him."

"About a half second, I'd say."

"Well, who's counting? Now get going. We've some riding to do."

Rivers started to salute, then realized that Cody wasn't in uniform and awkwardly dropped his arm. He trotted off to climb the hill he had just come down, and ran right through a pair of buzzards that flapped and squawked as they hopped out of his way.

Scofield came up, panting for breath. He looked at the dead men in disbelief.

"Colonel Cody, sir, I never saw anything like it."

"Like what?"

"Like the shooting you did. I had a bird's eye view and saw those three men buck up against you. I thought sure you were a goner."

Zak said nothing as he holstered his pistol, then lifted it slightly to keep it loose.

"I mean, how do you do that, sir?" Scofield said.

"What?"

"Go up against three gunmen and come out without nary a scratch? I couldn't see your hand real well, but I know it was empty when that fat one went for his gun."

"It's real simple, Corporal. I knew what he was going to do. He didn't know what I was going to do."

"That simple?"

"Almost. Near enough."

"Yes, sir. Mighty fine shooting, though."

"Scofield, these men are dead. They didn't have to die. I gave them a choice. They picked the wrong one. I regret that I had to kill them. I feel sorry for the lives they gave up."

"Well, they were trying to kill you, sir."

"Yes, they were. But I walked into their world. I was the intruder, not they. Makes you wonder."

"What's that, sir?"

"Just what keeps the world in balance. A man swats at a bug, kills it with the palm of his hand. Another cuts off a snake's head, while another shoots quail out of the sky. Who keeps track of such small things? And what does it mean when the final count is tallied? Nothing? Or everything?"

"I don't follow you, sir."

"No need, Scofield. I just hate to take a life. It leaves an empty hole in the life of someone who's still living. And maybe it leaves a little hole in my life, too."

"Aw, you can't go worrying about trash like these, sir. They was rawboned killers. Probably got more blood on their hands than you got on your hankie when you was a nose-bleedin' kid."

"Let's go, Scofield," Zak said. "Rivers will bring your horse and Miss O'Hara to the high end of that hill, and we'll get on the trail of Trask and Ferguson. You want to ride double?"

"I'll walk, sir, if it's all the same to you."

Scofield looked at the dead men again and shook his head as if he were still trying to figure it all out. The buzzards flapped, and three more landed some fifty yards away. They were ringed by the scavengers now and there were more still floating in the sky, their circles getting smaller as they slowly descended toward earth.

The smell of death lingered in Zak's nostrils a long time that day. He was glad that Colleen didn't say anything about what he'd done, although he'd bet a day's pay that Rivers told her all about it, no doubt in exaggerated terms.

"I'm sorry," she said that night when they stopped by a dry wash to rest the horses and stretch their legs.

"About what?"

"About what you had to do today. I know it was necessary."

"It wasn't necessary, Colleen. It was brutal and cruel and heartless."

"But—"

"No, that's what it was. I'm glad you weren't around to see it."

"You're awful hard on yourself, Zak."

He didn't say anything for a long time. She moved in closer to him and he could smell her scent, her soft womanly scent, like lilacs and mint growing under a cistern. Fresh and sweet. He wanted to kiss her, but Scofield and Rivers were watching them. This was not the time.

He wondered when that time would be.

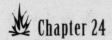 **Chapter 24**

Delbert Scofield finished smoking his cigarette, crushed it to bits between two fingers, scattered the remains on the ground. Then he scuffed up the dirt with his boot heels until there was no trace of tobacco or paper.

Hugo Rivers cleared his throat.

"When you aim to talk to Colonel Cody, Del?" he said.

Scofield looked over to where Colleen and Zak still stood.

"Directly. Soon as he gets finished sparking that schoolmarm."

"It just don't seem like he knows what for."

"He knows something, that's for sure."

"Look, we ain't follerin' the old stage road no more. We brung along all them horses what are slowin' us down. It don't seem like he's in no hurry to catch up with those outlaws we're supposed to be chasin'."

"I know. I wondered about that myself. And him goin' off by hisself ever' so often, ridin' up to the top of a hill and flashin' that little mirror."

"I ast him about that. He says it's a army helio-graph," Rivers said.

"A what?"

"A heliograph. It's got a little cross cut into it, so's he can sight the sun and make it bounce off. Says the Injuns call it a 'talkin' glass.' 'Spose he's talkin' to the Apaches?"

"I don't know what the hell he's doin', Hugo. This is gettin' to look more and more like a wild goose chase."

"Well, go ahead and ast him. We got a right to know. We're low on grub. He ain't said nothin' about beddin' down. He keeps lookin' at that sky gettin' blacker and blacker. We could get caught in a gully washer before mornin'."

"All right. Quit your bellyachin'. I'll ask him."

The horses, those that had belonged to Chama, Carmen, Julio, Manuel, and Renaldo, were all roped together, standing disconsolately a few feet away, their rumps to the north, as the sun died in the west below an ashen sky turning darker by the moment.

Bull bats knifed the air, scooping up insects, and a chill seemed to rise from the land as the shadows softened and melted together. An eerie stillness settled over the rocks and plants, the low hills.

"Time to mount up," Zak called over to Scofield and Rivers.

"Before we do, Colonel, sir, I got some questions, if that's all right."

"I have some questions of my own," Colleen said. "When you're finished asking, of course, Delbert."

"Yes'm."

"Corporal," Zak said.

"Yes, sir, well, sir, I just wanted to know why we're not trackin' them men. You left the old stage road, and they could be anywhere. Ain't nary a track out here in this open wilderness."

"I know where Trask and Ferguson are going, Scofield. I expect Miss O'Hara knows, too, don't you, Colleen?"

"Well, I know my brother makes maps. He wrote me what he was doing. He said he was marking where the Apache strongholds were, but only he can read the maps. He is probably guiding those men to one of the Apache camps, though. But I can't imagine that Ted would betray the Apaches he's made friends with. He . . . well, he said he respects them."

"I'm counting on that," Zak said.

"What about all that mirror flashing?" Scofield said. "You bringin' the Apaches down on us, maybe?"

Zak smiled. It was growing darker, but he could still see everyone's face, and they could see his.

"Tom Jeffords now knows we're coming. He'll tell Cochise, and we might be able to count on some Chiricahua help when we meet up with Trask and his bunch."

"Likely, the Apaches won't know the difference and wipe us all out," Rivers said.

"Shut up, Hugo," Scofield said. "I ain't finished with my questions yet." He paused, as if to collect his thoughts.

"Go on, Scofield," Zak said.

"Well, we got them horses what belonged to the people you killed, and they're slowin' us down. And we're about out of grub. We only brought enough to last us three until we got to Tucson."

"You'll find food in the saddlebags of those horses we brought along," Zak said. "And I have some in my own saddlebags. The horses are carrying bedrolls, water, rifles, and ammunition. They'll come in handy when we run into Trask. We're a few sleeps away from that, however."

"How long do you figure we'll be out here?"

"Oh, I expect we'll see Trask and Ferguson tomorrow. About the time that storm hits. They're riding the old stage road and I think they're going to stop at each station to see what I've done to Ferguson's operation. In fact, I'd say we're ahead of them now, and we should get a visit from Jeffords, and perhaps a few Apache braves, before dawn."

"So, you do have a plan," Scofield said.

Zak didn't answer. He turned to Colleen.

"You had some questions, Colleen?"

"I think you've answered most of them. I'm still wondering how you're—we're—going to save my brother, get him away from those awful men. I don't want him to be killed."

"I'm counting on your brother to make the right moves when we start the fight, Colleen. He's a smart man, and no doubt he's been looking for ways to escape all this time he's been in captivity. That's a bridge we'll cross when we come to it."

"Well, I worry."

"Well, don't. Worry is just something that keeps

you from thinking things through. It doesn't accomplish anything much, and it wears you down."

She gave out a small laugh.

"I see," she said.

"Look, all of you," Zak said, "I don't know what's going to happen. Trask is a dangerous man. A desperate man. I think the Chiricahua can help us. We're outgunned and outnumbered right now. But we hold some cards Trask doesn't know about. I think he's going to be surprised. I'm planning to make his hair stand on end."

There was a silence among them for several moments.

The sky blackened in the north and stars appeared to the east. The moon had not yet risen, but there were clouds blowing in over them and Zak knew they would likely see little of it during the night.

"Let's ride," Zak said. "From now on, every minute counts."

Scofield and Rivers walked to their horses. Colleen lingered. She put a hand on Zak's arm. There was a tenderness to her touch that stirred something inside him.

"I hope your plan works, Zak. For Ted's sake."

"Can you ride all night without falling off your horse, Colleen? We've a ways to go."

"Zak, I would ride anywhere with you. I want you to know that."

She squeezed his arm and moved closer to him. She tilted her head and he gazed down at her face. He could barely see it, but it seemed to him that her lips puckered slightly. He leaned down and brushed his lips against hers. She fell against him and he felt her trembling.

"I think I'm . . ."

He broke away, put a finger on her lips.

"Don't say it, Colleen. Not yet. Wait."

"Yes," she breathed, and he watched her walk away toward her horse.

He climbed onto Nox and took the lead, the others following close behind.

In the distance he heard the murmur of thunder, and when he looked back over his shoulder, he could see flashes of lightning in the black clouds. He rode into the darkness, thinking of Trask and how he had murdered his father. There would be a day of reckoning, he knew, for Trask and for him.

Then there was that blood sky of that morning. It carried a portent of much more than a storm. He took it as an omen, and he knew that was the Indian in him. Superstition. It could guide a man or defeat him. But the sky always spoke with a straight tongue.

There would be blood spilled on the morrow.

And the rain would wash it all back into the earth.

A coyote broke the stillness with its querulous call, its voice rising up and down the scale in a melodious and lonesome chant that was almost as old as the earth itself.

Nox whickered, and Zak patted him on the neck.

He felt his blood quicken and run hot.

"Trask," he whispered to himself, "I'm coming for you, you bastard."

Zak and his horse were shadows moving across

the dark land. Shadows as true and ominous as the bloody sunrise of **that** very morning.

Again the coyote called, but it was different this time.

The call came from a human throat.

An Apache throat.